Leave Nothing But Footprints

Patsy Collins

The author can be found at
www.patsycollins.co.uk

ISBN 978-1-914339-02-8

For my wonderful husband Gary Davies, who helped so much with the photographic aspects of this book and on whom none of Eliot's character traits are based.

Not even the occasional grumpiness.
Definitely not. At all. No way.

Chapter 1

"Come on, Jess, who is he and how did he break your heart?" Christina asked.

"And how can we help you get even?" Alyssa added.

"I told you, wanting a holiday on Capri and to spend time with my friends has nothing to do with a man," Jess said. That was true; almost. Eliot Beatty hadn't broken her heart, only disappointed her and not in the way they meant.

"So what is up?" Zoe asked.

Jess decided she might as well tell them. They cared and would ask until they got answers. "Nothing serious. It's college. I don't really get on with anyone and I'm not sure the course is right for me."

"There's something wrong with them if they don't get on with you," Christina said.

The others, bless them, nodded loyally.

"They're OK really, just young and…" Actually most of them did quite like her; or at least her generosity in the coffee shops and bakeries. They weren't real friends though and she felt uncomfortable around people so different from herself.

"It must be difficult going back into education after so long," Zoe said.

"It has been. Oh good, I think that's our drinks." Maybe her uneasiness was because she felt she was wasting time. At twenty-six, Jess was already ten years behind most of her fellow students and still not sure she was on the right track. One thing she did know was that coming to this beautiful island had been a good idea. Jess needed time to get over the setback of Eliot's rejection, and a break from her father's expectations, to consider how best to achieve the life she wanted. She was so pleased the others had agreed to accompany her to Capri. They'd been really lucky with the weather too. It was only April and yet they were sunbathing.

A slim waiter weaved his way through the sunbeds around the pool; the tray of cocktails held above head height, balanced on his fingertips. Sunlight lit up the drinks, making it look as though the glasses were prisms refracting its warm rays into jewel colours. Jess was sure the glasses were only held aloft to allow members of staff to move swiftly through the hotel guests without risk of brushing a uniformed elbow against oiled skin. The rainbow effect seemed all the more magical for being accidental.

As he delivered the Cosmopolitan, Blue Lagoon, Screwdriver and Grasshopper the waiter smiled at each girl in turn. "Enjoy your drinks, ladies," he said.

"Thank you," Jess said. Her Blue Lagoon, ordered in appreciation of the Blue Grotto they'd visited earlier that day, looked just as inviting as the cool water had after their flight. She hoped her photographs had done it justice.

"Thank you, Raoul," Christina said, managing to turn his name into a growl. That was kind of appropriate as although Christina wasn't old enough to be considered a cougar, she was looking at him as though he was prey.

"Wow," Alyssa said.

"They are huge." Zoe reached out a manicured hand to pick up the Grasshopper. "And so pretty." The rim of her glass had been dipped in cocoa. The brilliant green drink, the exact shade of her fingernails, was sprinkled with white chocolate chips and finished with a perfect sprig of mint.

"They are," agreed Alyssa. "But I was talking about the waiter. Did you see the way he managed to check us out and yet still seem polite?"

"Nope, I was too busy checking him out," Christina replied.

"No!" Zoe gasped. "Was he really?"

Jess laughed. "You lot never change."

"Here's to staying the same forever," Alyssa said.

All four girls clinked glasses.

As Jess took a sip of her drink she realised she was wrong; they had all changed from the carefree kids they'd been at school. Christina was occupied with her demanding career in accountancy, Alyssa her husband and charities, and Zoe's job, husband and three children kept her busy.

Her mother's illness had changed Jess too, into a responsible adult. After Mum's death she and her dad had grown closer than ever. She'd drifted into working for him before considering what she hoped to do with her life. Gradually she'd realised she was heading towards becoming a clone of her father and, much as she loved him, that didn't appeal in the slightest. It wasn't too late to create an alternative role for herself, as an influential photographer, but she probably had left it too long to return to education as though she were still sixteen.

For a while, the four girls shared memories of their schooldays, most of which seemed to involve what they'd got up to when they were supposed to be on cross-country runs. Then Zoe excused herself and headed back into the hotel.

As soon as she was out of earshot, Christina said, "I'm worried about her, financially I mean. Frankly, when you suggested this trip, Jess, I doubted she'd be able to afford it. I offered to chip in a bit if she couldn't, but she said there was no need and was so embarrassed I let it drop."

"I haven't liked to say anything, but I wondered too," Alyssa said. "She's only choosing things which are covered in the all-inclusive package. Just a single colour nail varnish, not the patterned or tipped options the rest of us opted for. Maybe it's what she wants, but I think she's trying to keep her costs down."

Jess hadn't noticed. Zoe had always been the least flamboyant, most conservative of them. When they'd bought masses of ultra fashionable clothes she'd stuck with her classic outfits, when they splashed out on loads of sweets at the cinema's pick 'n' mix counter, she'd claimed to be concerned about spots and went without. She'd also had the least money of them all.

"I'll have a word, if you like," Jess said. "Make sure she's OK."

Now she thought about it she realised Zoe had joined them for the massage which was complimentary but declined the hot stone treatment which wasn't, saying she preferred to keep it traditional. When the others had taken a yoga class she'd said she'd find lazing in the shade finishing her book more relaxing. Maybe that was true, but Jess didn't like the idea that her friend might not be enjoying the trip as much as she could due to concerns over money.

"So, that's her sorted, now what about you?" Alyssa asked Jess.

Jess sometimes thought her own problems were partly

financial too, though in her case the issue was having too much without the satisfaction of earning it. But as she had no intention of giving up the generous allowance her father gave her, and not purely because of how he'd react, perhaps she should stop trying to pretend his money was a disadvantage.

Tanya, a girl on her college course, had made that accusation. She'd also said Jess had a tendency to make everything all about her. Tanya had a point. Rather than allowing herself to enjoy the luxurious pampering the spa offered, Jess compared procedures designed to remove hair, suck out fat and pump in nutrients with the treatments which had tried, and failed, to save her mother. The unhappiness this brought was marring the trip for the others.

She looked at her friends concerned faces and gave herself a mental shake. "I'm fine, honestly I am," Jess said. Of course she was happy, but hiding things wouldn't convince them of that. "Sorry, it's just that I've been thinking of Mum. When she was ill someone came in and did our nails and hair. She'd have loved it here. And I love being here with all of you."

Zoe was back in time to hear the end of that and join in the group hug.

As they drank their cocktails, the other three persuaded Jess to explain how she'd come to start her college course. "I've been interested in photography for ages."

"Interested in a photographer, you mean!" Christina said.

"That's right. You had some mad crush on a guy who worked for your dad. What was his name?" Zoe asked.

"Eliot Beatty," Jess said. "He didn't work for Dad exactly and I…"

"Oh! I didn't realise it was him," Christina said. "No wonder you had a thing for him. He's gorgeous."

"What you mean is he's male!" Jess teased. "OK I did have a bit of a crush on him when I was twelve, but I haven't seen him since." She remembered him as slightly thin and a bit spotty, yet still good looking. He'd been charming to her too and made her feel like a real person, rather than Daddy's little girl. That was something which never happened in her father's presence and probably the main reason for her crush. It sounded as though Eliot was even more attractive now.

"Anyway, after Dad got engaged to Lizzie I realised I had to do something with my own life. Photography was the only thing which appealed and I tried to get Eliot Beatty to help. Dad had helped him with his career so it seemed only fair. Plus he'd been sweet to me when I was a kid."

"Something tells me he isn't being sweet now," Alyssa said.

"Not particularly, but there's no reason he should."

Jess hadn't forgotten her earlier feelings for Eliot when she'd thought of contacting him, but it was his talent she was really interested in. She'd started by looking at his website to see if he offered instruction. She learned he used to but had since stopped. The website gave a list of others who did offer that service. Jess hadn't clicked those links; she hoped she wouldn't need to.

There was very little actual information about the man behind the lens and no photo of him. Eliot's website was simply a showcase of his work, which she already knew was brilliant, and a subtle advertisement for the projects he was interested in. It was abundantly clear he was an environmentalist and nature lover. That was something they had in common in a way; Jess always bought environmentally friendly products, recycled everything, and adored wild flowers.

She'd emailed, asking for his help. Jess mentioned her GCSE grades and admitted she wasn't sure exactly what kind of photography she wanted to do, although she had ruled out joining the celebrity obsessed paparazzi. Maybe he could suggest what would be the best way for her to make a difference in the world?

The reply, when it eventually came, felt very like a standard, and slightly dismissive, response. He gave her links to photographers who offered training in areas such as landscape, portraits and wedding photography, saying that it had taken each of them years to learn the techniques and develop their skills. If she was serious about becoming a photographer then she should take a course – perhaps something general which would give her an idea of which area she'd like to focus on.

At first she'd been disappointed both that he hadn't remembered her and that he'd treated her like a schoolgirl who didn't know what she wanted to do when she grew up. After rereading her own message she could understand it. For one thing, she'd just signed it 'Jess' and her email address was one she'd created as a teenager, 'no-mess-wiv-jess'. No wonder he hadn't realised who she was and had assumed she was sixteen. She really must set up something more adult!

She told herself there was no reason he should have remembered her even if she'd signed herself as Jessica Borlase. Naturally he'd remember Daddy and might have wanted to help his daughter, but he didn't owe Jess anything. That was good, she almost convinced herself. He'd given her unbiased advice. Why not take it?

"So," Jess rounded off the explanation to her friends, "I signed up for the media studies course at the local college. That was maybe a bit too general. We're starting the photography module on Monday, which involves a visit to Eliot Beatty's latest exhibition. After that, I'm not sure if it's worth me staying on."

"Maybe after that you won't need to?" Alyssa said.

"How do you mean?"

"You can't tell us you weren't hoping for a bit more of a personal response from Eliot Beatty," Zoe prompted.

"I admit I was, but… Oh, you think he'll be there?"

"And see you've grown up to be totally gorgeous and serious about photography and whisk you away on some exotic shoot where you can see what develops? Yes, exactly," Christina said.

"Get your own fantasies, you lot! Now, are we having our next cocktail before or after dinner?"

"After. It's getting cool out here," Zoe said.

"It is a bit. See you all down in the restaurant in half an hour?" Jess suggested.

On the way back to their rooms they passed through the foyer where a selection of magazines was on offer. The front cover of one promised 'Eliot Beatty up close and personal', so Jess bought it and flicked through as she waited for the lift. The article had no more personal information than the few details she'd read on his website, but it did have a large photograph of the man himself. Wow!

Jess inspected her own appearance in the mirror of her suite. Oh dear, definitely not close-up ready! She'd had her hair blow-dried earlier, but the moist air by the pool had made it start to frizz up again and her make-up was smudged from laughing so much. As she sorted out her eyeliner and straightened her hair, Jess thought about what Zoe and the others had said about her hopes for a different reaction from Eliot. Even if she hadn't been then, she was now. In fact, her thoughts had become so Christina-esque that she was late leaving her room to meet the others and then absent-mindedly went the wrong way, so arrived breathless from somewhere she perhaps shouldn't have been. Not surprisingly, her candid explanation resulted in plenty of teasing.

"If he can get you this worked out just from thinking about him, imagine what he could do in the flesh," Christina said.

"I'm not going to just imagine," Jess replied. "I plan to find out."

Chapter 2

"Bliss," Zoe said as her meal was placed in front of her.

"We haven't even tasted it yet," Alyssa pointed out. "Although come to think of it, that does mean we haven't had to cook it."

"Exactly. Plus none of it looks like fish fingers or will get smothered in ketchup."

"It does look good," Jess said. "Which makes three of us appreciating our meals and one far more interested in the man in tight trousers who carried it out from the kitchen."

"Hey! I'm not a complete tart you know!" Christina said. "Well, not so much it puts me off my food." She speared a juicy king prawn coated in chili and garlic sauce. "Come here you tasty little chap."

"Would madam care for pepper?" The waiter, Raoul who'd attended them by the pool, had reappeared at Christina's side with perfect timing.

Christina's flirtatious remark that she'd like anything he had to offer was almost drowned out by the giggles of her friends. She gave a hugely dramatic sigh as he sauntered away from the table.

"Stop playing with the staff and eat your food like a good girl," Alyssa said.

Christina stuck out her tongue, then followed the advice.

Jess too concentrated on her meal. It was such a pleasure to order whatever she liked the sound of, rather than having to carefully visualise each dish in advance or risk being faced with something she just couldn't eat. She was delighted the spa's restaurant had fully embraced the low carb trend. No white bread, rice, potatoes or pasta were provided as standard with the meals, although they could be ordered as an extra. Instead, a tempting array of brightly coloured salads and attractively cut and presented vegetables accompanied the dishes. Meat, fish or nuts were marinated in red wine or coated in vibrant sauces. In place of heavy puddings, guests were served delicate slivers of fruit on polished slates. The dark background and reflected candlelight gave the impression of tiny stained glass windows. Jess was glad she'd left her camera in her room when they'd got dressed for dinner, as she'd have been tempted to photograph everything before they ate.

Over after-dinner drinks the friends discussed what they'd do the following day.

"I've seen some fantastic images of the island's rock formations," Jess said. "I'd like to see if I can take similar pictures." She used her phone to access the internet and show the others what she had in mind, including the famous natural arch and Siren's rock.

"Looking at the scenery sounds good to me," Zoe said.

The other two declared themselves happy with anything which didn't require too much walking up the rocky island's many flights of steps, and ended up with cocktails by the pool.

"Shall we hire a boat for the day?" Jess suggested. "That way we'll see everything and I'll be able to get into good positions for photography."

"And Christina will be able to get into naughty positions with the crew."

Christina countered with, "And Alyssa won't have to make the ultimate sacrifice of wearing sensible footwear instead of shoes which make it seem she intends to spend more time on her back than her feet."

Alyssa did her best to hide a laugh with a scowl. "Don't judge my Louboutins by your libido!"

"Actually, I don't think I'll come," Zoe said.

"Hey, we were just kidding!"

"Course we were, even though I'm right," Alyssa agreed.

"I know that, but I think I'll stay here and top up my tan."

"Oh go on, come with us, Zoe." Alyssa put her own phone on the table and scrolled through details of Capri. "There's a green grotto. I want to see if that matches your nails as well as Jess's drink and the blue grotto matched hers."

As Alyssa was talking, Christina, unseen by Zoe, rubbed her fingers and thumb together. Jess nodded to show she understood the gesture meant Alyssa suspected Zoe's reluctance was due to the cost.

When Zoe said, "Perhaps you could photograph it for me?" Jess was sure that was the case.

"Of course I will. Actually I'd like to take a picture of us now, see if I can get a night shot to work. I'll nip up and get my camera."

"You won't get lost again will you?" Christina said. "If you do, I'll have to get that dishy waiter to come with me and look for you in some very unlikely places."

Before Jess could ask Zoe to come with her, she offered

to do that herself.

On the way to Jess's room, Zoe said, "I'm not sure I'll be much help, my sense of direction is no better than yours."

"Ah well, at least I'll have someone to talk to while we wander round in circles… although I suspect you offered to get away from the conversation about the boat trip?"

"You know what Christina's like when she gets an idea; won't let it drop. I'm seriously worried for that poor waiter."

"Ha! Me too. But you don't get to change the subject that easily. Do you really not fancy the boat trip?"

"I do… but I can't afford it, Jess. It'll get better soon, but at the moment everything we have is going to pay the mortgage and a savings scheme for the kids' education. It was fantastic of you to pay for this trip for me and I'm really, really grateful."

"Stop that. I said you'd be doing me a favour by coming and I meant it. Having my old friends around me was important right now and I appreciate you taking time away from your kids and work. Because of that, I want you to have a really good time. We all do."

"Thanks, Jess. That's so sweet of you."

"So come on the boat trip? We're hiring the thing anyway, so it won't cost any more for you to join us."

Jess could see her friend was tempted. "Please. We need a responsible adult in case Christina really does take a fancy to the captain of our boat."

"OK. Thanks, Jess. For everything."

The boat trip, and the rest of the holiday was a success. Jess left with lots of photos, a more definite vision for her future and the confidence she could succeed in her chosen career.

A week later, at Eliot Beatty's 'Before and After' exhibition, Jess stopped at a life-size photographic montage of a naked man. His arms were outstretched, almost as though nailed on a cross. In one half of the image he was naked. The other side showed him wearing a business suit and holding a briefcase. He was clean shaven, hair neatly combed, hands-free phone around his ear. The naked side was bearded with straggly hair. In his hand was soil with a seedling sprouting from it. The backgrounds were different too. The naked man stood in front of a green landscape. The City gent was backed by a polluted urban jungle.

Jess knew she should be studying the image as a whole and absorbing the message, or learning something about the techniques used to create it, but all she could do was gaze into the dark-lashed eyes of Eliot Beatty. He was undeniably attractive but there was something unsettling about him too.

"Hmm, I'm beginning to see the advantages of photography," Tanya said. "Wouldn't mind him modelling for me!"

"No, er, yes."

"Oh come on, you're not trying to tell me the only technique he could interest you in is Photoshop?"

"OK, he is pretty gorgeous."

"So, you're human after all?"

"Didn't you think I was?" Jess asked.

"Oh I knew it, just wasn't sure you did. Everyone acts like you're sooo special just because you've got cash to spare, but being able to buy the best of everything doesn't make you better." Although her words were bitter her tone wasn't.

Jess remembered expressing surprise that Tanya didn't simply replace her slow laptop with the latest model, or get a taxi instead of waiting in the cold for unreliable buses. It was hard to say whether Tanya was more upset before or after she realised Jess wasn't being sarcastic, or bragging about her own wealth.

"So, I'm a snob who flashes her cash too much. Anything else you don't like about me?"

Tanya grinned. "Oh tons. I'm jealous of your perfect grades. Mine are rubbish next to yours. That doesn't make you better either. Like to see how you'd manage in an overcrowded council flat instead of the east wing in Daddy's mansion."

Jess didn't say she actually lived in an apartment in her father's spacious seafront town house. She guessed Tanya, rightly, wouldn't be moved to pity by the difference. Jess transferred her attention to the next set of photos and sighed. They were just as brilliant as all the others, making her realise how poor her own efforts were. She'd taken quite a few snaps on Capri, but that's just what they were; snaps. The trip had both comforted and unsettled her. The other girls had careers or families and their lives sorted. Jess had only recently decided what she wanted to do and was no nearer achieving it than were the sixteen-year-olds she studied with.

Her tutor said Jess was one of his best students. That was probably true as she was one of the few who handed in any work. Take this exhibition for instance; Jess and Tanya were the only two who'd stayed once he'd marked them down as present. The rest almost ran through the rooms before heading for the nearest coffee shop.

Jess hadn't been ready to leave. The sheer beauty of some of Eliot Beatty's images made her long to stand and stare at them. Others were of more interest because of their power to provoke an emotional response.

"You all right?" Tanya asked.

"Just thinking."

"Not about the snidey bitch with a chip on her shoulder you're stuck with?"

"About photography. What do you think of this?" Jess indicated a photo. "If it'd been taken a few weeks earlier, the scene would have been much prettier. I doubt he just got there a bit late but decided to include it anyway." The photograph showed a well-lit glade of beech trees and swathe of bluebells. The bulbs had finished flowering, the foliage was yellow and floppy.

They read the accompanying notice which, as with the other images, stated when and where it had been taken and explained the equipment and techniques used to produce it. In this case there was a choice of titles. Either 'Another Spring Missed' or 'Summer's Approach'.

"Which would you pick?" Jess asked.

"Feels like a personality test; 'are you an optimist?' Even so, I'm going for 'Summer's Approach'."

"Me too."

They studied the photo and decided that, unlike the other images which were intended to show the damage man was doing to nature, this seemed to question people's attitudes to its beauty. Jess saw that the seed heads of the bluebells were green and fat, almost ready to increase the number of flowers for future years. The canopy of fresh new beech leaves and elephant-hide tree trunks were shown to be important, rather than merely a foil for the fleeting flowers.

Pink campion, which would have contrasted beautifully

with the bluebells, was still blooming. Clumps of other wild flowers, which would bring colour later in the year, pushed through the decay. Queen Anne's lace, buttercups and meadow cranesbill, Jess thought. Perhaps earlier in the year there had been snowdrops, wood anemones and wild garlic. She'd like to go there herself, to see if she was right and to photograph the changes through the seasons. She checked the catalogue for details of the location, learning nothing more than that it was somewhere in South Wales.

"It's better to have someone to discuss the work with, isn't it?" Jess said as they moved onto the next image.

"Maybe." Tanya didn't sound convinced. "Not much to discuss, is there? Just the same old, same old."

"How do you mean?" Jess had seen examples of excellent photography. Maybe by studying them she'd get some clues about employing the techniques she'd read about but had little success with.

"It's the old shock and awe. Recycle or die. People are always bad. Progress is always bad. Everything's black and white."

"Except for the yellow, cyan and magenta?" She named three of photography's key colours.

Tanya turned away, but not before Jess saw her suppress a grin.

"Images are like that, aren't they? They're supposed to be dramatic," Jess asked.

"Yeah, but it's all too much. It puts me off to know the polar ice caps are melting and thousands of creatures are going extinct," Tanya indicated pictures making just those points. "There's nothing I can do about it, you know?"

"I suppose there isn't much we can do individually, but seeing the problem reminds people to try to do something."

"Do something, or make a donation?"

"What else can I do?"

Tanya shook her head. "You? Nothing, I'm sure."

Jess stepped in front of the other girl. "What are you implying?"

Tanya put up her hands in surrender. "Forget it. It's not your fault you've got a rich father and I haven't got one at all."

They continued on to the next display board. The two of them were very different, but Tanya was still walking by her side. If she were to reach out perhaps the younger girl would respond. It was worth a try. "Is photography what you're hoping to do after college?"

"What I want is to make enough to live on, so I don't have to share a flat with my mum and stepdad, and a bedroom with my baby sister. They're great in small doses, but they do my head in."

"I can understand that. My dad is getting married again." Talking to Tanya was making Jess feel more grateful for her advantages than usual. Lizzie wasn't great even in the tiniest of doses, but thankfully she'd not reproduced, and Jess wasn't forced to live with her.

"What about you then, what are your plans?" Tanya asked.

"I'm not sure in which field, but I do want to be a photographer. One who makes a difference. I've read up on it and I've practised a lot away from college."

"Yeah. I see you've done more than just bought the gear. So being a weather presenter is out then?"

"Definitely!"

They both chuckled at the memory of one girl who had

that ambition and complained Jess had such an unfair advantage over her; she had the wardrobe for the job.

Tanya took a deep breath as though preparing herself for something. "Actually I was thinking maybe I could work in TV myself."

"Really?" That didn't fit with what she knew of Tanya, but then Jess didn't know her well.

"Not in front of the camera, I don't mean. I was thinking of applying to be a researcher. You know, gathering the opinions of ordinary people, checking facts, collecting data. I like finding things out."

Jess nodded. "I can imagine you doing that." Some of the other students simply googled for homework answers and copied down the first entry they found without checking if it was accurate. Tanya never made that mistake. However brief her responses, they were always correct.

The girls studied another series of landscapes. Eliot had created two images of each location. The flat expanse of moor, verdant woodland and deserted beach were very slightly blurry, as if in romantic soft focus, or viewed through a steamy window. This gave the impression they were slipping away from the view never to be seen again. In the foreground of each was a single item in sharp focus. For half of them it was a delicate wild flower, ladybird or a perfect shell. The sister image featured a decomposing gull caught in tangled line, a dead stag its magnificent antlers caught in a shopping trolley, and a hedgehog trapped in a tin can.

"See, shock and awe," Tanya said.

"But that really happens."

"True, but d'you need to see them to know you shouldn't drop litter?"

"No, but others do."

"And they're the sort to go to photography exhibitions?"

Jess didn't answer because she knew Tanya was right. Instead she changed the subject. "I've got a confession to make."

"You're a family of space aliens whose ship was made of diamonds? That'd explain you being weird and rich."

"I think Dad would have mentioned that! No, it's just slightly less exciting. I know the photographer."

"Eliot Beatty? Really? How?"

"He's my dad's protégé. I don't know all the details, but my father discovered Eliot had talent but no money so provided enough to get him started. I haven't seen him since I was a little kid but I did meet him a couple of times. He photographed me actually."

"Daddy provided the money! Now I'm jealous of Mr Beatty too."

"Tanya, I…"

"Don't worry, I only half mean it and I'm not going to try to get your old man to sponsor me or anything."

Jess smiled in the hope of showing she'd not suspected Tanya of anything like it.

An elderly man, wearing a pass around his neck and carrying a radio, approached. "Excuse me, ladies, but I'm afraid I must ask you to leave. The exhibition has now closed for the evening."

They apologised and headed for the exit. On their way out, Jess said, "I didn't realise we'd been there so long. I'm famished. Fancy getting a Chinese or something?"

"Sorry, I'm skint. Maybe another time?"

"My treat. I'm not being patronising," she added when she saw Tanya's expression. "I always buy way too much and waste half of it." She could see Tanya was tempted. "Please. There's no one at home and I'd like some company."

Tanya checked her watch. "Wish I could. I lurve Chinese food, but I've got to babysit my sister. Mum's working tonight."

"A quick coffee then?"

"Sure."

They both ordered cappuccinos.

"I'll get these," Tanya said. Her tone discouraged Jess from arguing.

Once sitting with their drinks, Jess recounted what she remembered about Eliot. Her more distant memories were perhaps coloured by the recent photos she'd seen of him, as her account was both detailed and enthusiastic.

"If he's so nice perhaps he'd give you some advice?" Tanya said.

"That's what I've been thinking," Jess said.

She'd finally made friends with Tanya after a less than perfect start. She could easily do the same with Eliot Beatty; in his case, she wouldn't be starting off with the disadvantage that he considered her a spoilt little madam. All she had to do was get to meet him and turn on the irresistible Borlase charm.

Chapter 3

Jess let herself into her home. She looked around at the tidy apartment. The floors were pale wood throughout and the walls painted cream to give a spacious feel. That had been her thought when she'd instructed the decorators, but after hearing about Zoe's life with her children, and Tanya's home, Jess realised she really did have a lot of space. A living room, bathroom, bedroom, kitchenette, sound-proofed office and utility area all to herself was more than many people had. Far more. She even had her own tiny walled garden where she grew the wild flowers her mum had taught her to love. Tanya didn't even have her own bedroom, where she could work quietly away from the rest of her family. No wonder she was jealous of everything Jess took for granted.

After kicking off her shoes, Jess walked across her soft turquoise rug. She'd had that made specially because she couldn't find one which was just right to match the turquoise bed linen, sofa, towels and even tea towels. The effect was very neat, stylish, but rather empty. She hadn't wanted a cluttered look and requested the planners include plenty of storage and box in all the cables to give a sleek finish. They'd achieved that, but now it all looked barren.

With her bookcases behind flush fitting doors and even her camera equipment neatly stowed away, the only personal items on show were her discarded shoes, her coat thrown onto the sofa and a portrait on the wall. When Jess came in tomorrow the coat and shoes, if she weren't wearing them, would have been put away by Mrs Jennings. Even the portrait of Daddy was a formal studio one, not a candid shot taken at a family event, or one she'd taken herself.

Jess threw herself down on the sofa and hugged one of the turquoise cushions to her chest. What on earth was wrong with her? She should be content. When the others at college helped spend her money it seemed to make them happy for a short time. If Tanya had this much space to work she'd be delighted. If Tanya, Zoe, Alyssa or Christina had the weekend free they'd probably be pleased too, not desperately searching for ways to fill the time.

Jess had a lovely home, caring father, plenty of money. She knew she should be grateful, and she was, yet still felt dissatisfied. There must be something more meaningful she could hope for. Not marriage – she'd decided against that. She had a pretty face, decent figure and, she thought, a nice personality but imagined she'd get just as much male attention without any of that. All anyone seemed to see was her money, unless they had plenty themselves and then it was their money which concerned them. Her father was so keen to fix her up with a son of one of his friends, and those friends equally eager, that she felt like a brood mare. That's all they really wanted, someone to carry on the family name and inherit their money. Daddy had suggested she join her name to her husband's rather than just taking his, even before she'd been on her first date.

The nearest Jess had come to rebelling against her father was refusing to fall in love with any of the 'suitable' young men she was introduced to. She wouldn't fill her days supervising the nanny and planning elaborate dinner parties. She'd persuaded her father to let her return to education rather than continue as his assistant, but the media studies course had been a compromise. She'd have preferred a purely photographic course; he wanted one which would keep her options open and be of use if she continued to work for him, as he assumed she would.

Jess needed something to care about without the risk of getting hurt and was more sure than ever that photography was the answer. Now she'd made that decision, she'd be better off leaving college and concentrating on photography. If she could persuade Eliot Beatty to teach her, and she was confident she could, that would be perfect. She could learn more from him than from all the books she'd bought on the subject and her college tutor combined. And perhaps as Christina had not so subtly suggested, it needn't be all work and no play.

She again visited his website. It had been updated with the details of his 'Before and After' exhibition. There was also a recorded interview with Eliot. She felt the tension in it as she listened. Eliot had clearly only taken part as a way to promote a clean-up project which he hoped to get more people and businesses involved in. The interviewer, equally as clearly, wanted gossip about the famous people he mixed with, and his own love life.

Eliot spoke warmly about those celebrities who openly cared about the world around them and acted as good role models.

'So, if people turn up to collect rubbish on the beach next week, will they meet anyone famous?' the interviewer asked.

'They will and they'll probably get photographed by me for the papers, but hopefully that won't be their whole reason for taking part.'

Getting involved might be a way to reach Eliot and convince him she was on his wavelength. Jess paused the playback to check the date of the interview. It was weeks old, so too late for her to join the volunteers and meet him that way. She pressed play.

After prompting, which bordered on harassment, Eliot admitted to knowing several very attractive and famous women, but seemed as interested in their green credentials as their figures and availability.

'So no wedding bells, or any need for a girl to give up hope?' the interviewer asked in a flirtatious tone.

'I'm married to my work.'

'That doesn't sound encouraging.'

'It wasn't supposed to,' Eliot retorted.

Jess couldn't help giggling; he'd sounded just like she must when some chinless wonder couldn't seem to understand that she wasn't just playing hard to get and really didn't want to go out with him. Just as Jess did with sons of her father's business friends, Eliot had to be reasonably polite to the media.

She wondered if Eliot had written a photography book. If he had it would probably be far more readable than those she already had; no doubt they all contained useful information, but Jess hadn't yet found the time or concentration to really study them. There was no mention of one on his website and an Amazon search revealed only books containing his photographs. There were lots of those, but he hadn't written any of them.

Before she could place an order, there was a tap on her door. When she opened it, her father was standing in her hallway. "You're late, Pumpkin," he said.

"Oh sorry. I'd have phoned if I'd known you'd be home already."

"That's all right. I've just got back myself and thought I'd come down and see if you'd like a drink with me."

"Just you, Daddy?"

"Would it make a difference?"

Of course it made a difference. Surely he understood she'd rather talk to him on his own than try to make polite conversation with his fiancée. "I just wondered."

"Just me. Lizzie is out with some friends."

"Ah. Yes, I'd like to come up for a drink. Just give me five minutes, will you?"

After Jess had hastily smoothed down her hair and applied fresh lipstick, she went up to her father's part of the house. They settled into his den and Aubrey Borlase poured a glass of Tia Maria for his daughter and a malt whisky for himself.

"So, what have you been up to this evening? Out with your college friends?" He made it sound as though they were all six and had been playing on the swings.

"We went to an exhibition this afternoon, as part of the course. I had coffee with one of the girls afterwards. Tanya and I talked about the careers we're aiming for. She's hoping to become a researcher for the BBC."

"That sounds sensible. Much better than these kids who think all they've got to do is wiggle their hips and they'll be a celebrity. No talent at all some of them."

"Yes, Daddy." Jess humoured him as he started on one of his favourite themes. After a while she changed the subject. "The exhibition I went to was by Eliot Beatty."

"Ah, now that boy does have talent. I recognised it right off. He'd still have got somewhere even without my backing, but I'm proud of what I did to help."

"Yes and I expect he's grateful." Hopefully grateful enough to do the same for her.

Aubrey beamed. "How's your course going? Working

out all right? If it's not what you want to do we can find you another, or maybe you'd like to travel, eh?"

Jess was pretty sure that travelling was one of Lizzie's ideas.

"It's been useful in helping me be certain about what I want to do, but I think I've got everything out of it that I'm going to. Daddy, you remember I said I want to be a photographer?"

"Yes, Pumpkin. Do you need a new camera?"

"No, Daddy. I don't want to do it as a hobby, but professionally just like Eliot Beatty does. His work is important. It makes people think and it gets things done. He helps promote environmental concerns. I'd love to do the same kind of thing."

"Hmmm, not the career I was thinking of for you."

"It is what I want. I've always been interested, you know that, and I'm getting better all the time." She told him how much she'd improved by following the advice in the photography magazines she'd subscribed to, and that the photography module in college had helped too. "With the proper instruction, right equipment and plenty of practice then maybe I could get really good. Perhaps hold exhibitions myself."

That last bit was said mainly to appeal to her father's vanity. He'd sponsor her she knew and make sure she got good press coverage, which would make him proud of her.

"I helped set up young Beatty and I won't do any less by my own daughter. What do you need? How about a studio, will you need to set one up?"

"No, nothing like that. I'll need training though and then work where I can gain experience and maybe start to build a reputation."

"Then Eliot Beatty is the man you need, Pumpkin. I'll have a little chat with him."

"Thanks, Daddy, but there's no need for that." Jess kissed her father goodnight and returned to her own rooms.

She emailed Eliot again, using her old email address as her new one included her surname. If she hoped to get Eliot to take her seriously, she couldn't hide behind her father.

This time Jess thought carefully about her email and didn't just type the first thing which came into her head. She rejected her first attempt as too formal and grovelling and tried again.

Hi Eliot,

I emailed you a while ago, asking for advice about a career in photography. You suggested I take a course – I did, so thanks for that. It's in media studies and we've just done the photography module. My grades were pretty good. As part of the course we went to your 'Before and After' exhibition. It was amazing. I love anything to do with nature, especially wild flowers and you really showed how important it is that we protect wild places.

I'm more sure than ever that photography is definitely what I want to do and I think I'll be good at it, especially if I have the right training. As you don't offer tuition, I've been thinking that what would be really good is a kind of internship, unpaid of course, so I can work with and learn from you for a few weeks.

Best wishes,

Jess.

That was better, putting them as equals and showing she wasn't expecting something for nothing. To show she would be useful she added details about the camera equipment she had – which was all absolutely top of the range. Jess considered mentioning the donation she'd made to the wildlife charity Eliot's exhibition was supporting but decided against it. As Tanya had hinted, using her iPad to transfer a thousand pounds was the same as others dropping a few coins into the collecting boxes. Besides, that was Daddy's money and she was determined to gain Eliot's help herself.

His reply came through a couple of days later, when Jess was leaving college for lunch. She read it twice, wondering if she'd somehow misunderstood.

Dear Jess,

Thank you for your kind words about the exhibition.

As I'm sure I will have explained in any previous communication, it takes time and hard work to learn the techniques and develop the skills required to become a professional photographer. I couldn't pass that onto someone in a few weeks even if I wanted to. My reluctance to make the attempt is why I no longer offer training courses. Many of my colleagues do and I've attached a list of those I recommend you consider.

I don't feel that you would benefit from an internship with me and at the risk of sounding harsh, the assistance of an untrained person, no matter how enthusiastic and potentially skilled, is not something which would be of use to me. In order to be clear, I have no requirement for an employee, whether paid or unpaid, in any capacity whatsoever.

You are extremely fortunate to have such excellent photographic equipment. That alone won't make you a good photographer, but as long as you take the trouble to learn to use it correctly, a good camera is an asset. I encourage you to use yours at every opportunity and to study the results critically. By making mistakes and learning from them, you are sure to improve.

Regards,

Eliot Beatty

"Are you OK?" Tanya asked.

"No I'm not! How could he be so rude? He says it wouldn't help me, but clearly he hasn't even thought about it from my point of view."

"Who hasn't thought about what?"

"Eliot Beatty. Look at what I sent and how he replied."

Tanya took Jess's phone. After a moment she said, "I can see it isn't the answer you wanted, but he hasn't been rude."

"Even when he says I'm no use to him?"

"You saw his photos. Do you really think he needs anyone else taking them for him?"

"No, but that's not the point."

"What is then?"

"I… well…"

"Come on," Tanya gestured toward the coffee shop.

"I'm perfectly calm, I don't need to sit down with a hot drink."

"No, but you owe me a coffee and I want you to pay for it before I say what I think you need to hear."

Jess took her purse from her bag, drew out a fiver and handed it to Tanya. "There, now tell me."

"OK, when was the last time you didn't get your way about something?"

"What do you mean?" Her life might seem easy to Tanya, but it was a struggle not to just be Daddy's little girl and fall in with his plans. She had Lizzie to contend with; her future stepmother pretended to have Jess's best interests at heart but she clearly had her own agenda. And Eliot certainly wasn't rushing to do her bidding.

"I wasn't having a go," Tanya said. "Just pointing out that things usually go your way. If you want something you buy it, if you want something done you hire someone to do it, if you want to go somewhere you book a ticket. You thought Mr Beatty would agree because that was what you wanted."

That wasn't quite fair, but Jess admitted she hadn't really considered the possibility of Eliot saying no. That perhaps was partly why she was so disappointed when he did. Partly it was because she'd been hoping for more than lessons. Spending time with him, improving her photographic skills was going to be just the first step in building a happy, fulfilling life for herself. It had seemed as though that vaguely imagined future had been snatched away before she'd clearly pictured it.

"You're right," Jess admitted. "I did assume he'd agree."

"So, now you know his answer, read the message again."

Jess did. Eliot hadn't really been as rude as she'd thought. Actually not rude at all, just unwilling to go along with her suggestion. Fine then, she'd accept that, but she still wanted to work with him, get to know him and… She wasn't going to give up that easily. She'd follow his advice, take one of the courses he'd suggested and then contact him again. This was a setback, not the end of her hopes.

First though, she was going to treat Tanya to a decent lunch and she would absolutely insist on having her way about that.

Chapter 4

As though to prove her point about her father continuing to run her life for her, a few days later he informed her he'd booked a table for seven-thirty in his favourite restaurant for the Friday evening. He didn't ask if she was free or even if she wanted to come. The nearest she got to having a say in anything was, "Would you like to travel with us, or meet us there?"

As 'us' meant him and Lizzie she opted for the latter.

Jess considered not bothering to change out of her college clothes as a protest at being bossed about, but decided that was childish. She showered, gave herself a quick facial and put her hair up, like the adult she was. Oddly that didn't feel any more like the real Jess than the loose ponytail, tight jeans and minimal make-up she wore in an attempt to fit in better with her younger classmates. Still, it would have to do. At least her cobalt blue, silk dress was distinctive. Alyssa had spotted a similar one when they went shopping for the Capri trip and said the style would be perfect for her.

"Yes, but not the colour," Jess had said. Fortunately the boutique had been happy to get a one-off made in any shade she chose and to her exact measurements.

When Jess was ready to leave, she discovered two taxis waiting. Her father had also booked one for her. She knew he meant well, but it was so frustrating that he never took seriously even her smallest attempts to become independent.

"Put an extra twenty pounds on the invoice for your inconvenience," she told the driver she sent away. She'd tip the other man just as much, but the extravagance wouldn't serve her father right; he wouldn't even see the bill as his PA dealt with all his minor accounts.

The first thing Jess noticed, as she walked into the restaurant, was the smug expression on Lizzie's face. That woman managed to spoil all Jess's time with her father, by insisting on accompanying him almost everywhere he went other than for work. She looked like she intended going a step further than simply being there this time. Jess crossed her fingers and hoped Lizzie wasn't about to announce she was pregnant.

Lizzie rose from the table and came to meet her.

"You look lovely, Jess," Lizzie said. "I love the way you've done your hair."

It always threw her when Lizzie said things like that. For her father's sake Jess tried to be polite. "You look nice too, Lizzie."

"Oh, thank you!" Lizzie looked as though she might hug her. Something in Jess's expression must have stopped her and she settled for a smile instead.

Perhaps Lizzie too was being polite for Daddy's sake and wasn't really being two-faced?

"Lovely to see you, Pumpkin," he said, as she bent to give him a kiss. "Lizzie is right, you do look nice."

She'd been right to make an effort with her appearance; if she hadn't, Daddy wouldn't have said anything, but he would have been disappointed.

"Come and sit down and tell me what you'd like to drink."

Obediently she sat beside him.

"Madeira, Pumpkin?"

"Actually, I think I'd rather have a G and T, Daddy." If Lizzie was about to make an appalling announcement then Jess didn't want to try to toast it with a sickly sweet drink. Much better to have a bigger glass to hide behind too.

"I'll have the same," Lizzie said.

Presumably she wouldn't drink if she was pregnant? What was this dinner about then? Belatedly Jess noticed the table was set for four. Was Lizzie conspiring with Daddy's attempts to set her up with 'a nice young man from the right kind of family'? To do her justice, Lizzie had never before tried to foist her off on the sons of Daddy's friends.

Jess couldn't help thinking of Tanya. Because the two of them were so different, Jess had misjudged her. It was just possible she'd done the same with Lizzie.

Thoughts of the other women were swept away by the sight of the most gorgeous man Jess had ever seen. It wasn't the first time she's seen him, but he was much better looking in real life than in the photograph she'd seen at the exhibition. This time he wasn't wearing a business suit, neither was he naked. He was perfectly dressed for the surroundings in a stylish blue shirt, tight fitting cream trousers and matching jacket. As he walked toward her, Jess couldn't help remembering how strong his thigh muscle had looked in the photograph and the way the dark hairs on his chest had seemed to invite her touch. The soft looking material of his trousers perfectly outlined the shape of his slim hips and he seemed to be making straight for Jess.

As though in a dream, the restaurant and her companions melted away, leaving just Jess and Eliot

Beatty. She didn't dare blink in case he disappeared and she discovered she was imagining him. Now she was seriously glad she hadn't given in to her petty impulse not to bother much about her hair and make-up before coming out.

The dream turned to nightmare as Lizzie rose to kiss his cheek. He gave her a brief hug and returned the kiss. The fact that Eliot was showing affection to Lizzie was seriously irritating, but nowhere near as annoying as the lack of surprise on her father's face. Jess had told him she'd speak to Eliot herself but he'd taken over as usual. Too bad for Daddy that she'd already asked and got her answer.

"Come on, I'll reintroduce you," Lizzie said to Eliot.

What gave her the right to act as hostess?

"You'll remember my fiancé Aubrey Borlase, of course. This is his daughter Jessica. Jess, dear I know you've met Eliot Beatty, but I don't think you've seen him for a while?"

Jess didn't answer. She didn't want her irritation to show and could hardly mention having seen him only a few days before and that he'd been half naked.

"I'm pleased to see you again, Jessica," Eliot said as though he meant it. He offered his hand. She placed hers in it and felt the warmth and strength of his handshake. Neither of them were in a hurry to let go.

"Isn't this where I'm supposed to embarrass you by saying the last time I saw you you were naked?" Eliot asked with a twinkle in his eye.

"What's that?" her father demanded.

"Just a joke, Mr Borlase. Jessica was such a little girl when I saw her last she could have been playing naked in a paddling pool or something when I visited."

She hadn't been quite young enough for that and temporarily she was frustrated that although she'd seen him as an attractive boy, he'd thought of her as just a kid. Then Eliot gave her a grin and a gentle squeeze of the hand he was still holding and she realised that, despite the emails, he didn't think that now. Jess blushed as she realised they were both thinking about the other being naked.

"Oh, yes, I see. Don't think she was though?"

"No, sir."

"Please, call me Aubrey, boy."

If Eliot minded being called 'boy' he didn't have time to show it before the waiter came to take their order. Jess managed to tear her attention away from Eliot just long enough to read out an almost random selection from the menu.

After they'd ordered, Eliot explained about his next major project as though he assumed that's why he'd been invited. For about a fortnight he'd be working in South Wales, mostly on the Pembrokeshire coast, photographing ecological success stories.

Hearing that, Jess was even more disappointed he'd said no to her suggestion she work with him. South Wales was beautiful and exploring the beaches with him sounded wonderful. With no one else for company, they'd get to know each other well and she was sure they'd soon become something more than just friends. She'd also learn a great deal about photography, Jess reminded herself.

"There's a lot of doom and gloom about the environment, I know because I've highlighted some of it in my work. The public are fed up with that and bad news about the economy and terrorism."

Jess nodded enthusiastically. She'd had the same

conversation at the exhibition. Tanya had made that point and Jess could now see she'd been right.

Eliot continued, "They'll respond to, and be inspired by, good news. Areas once full of litter have been cleaned up, beaches are being used responsibly, puffins are thriving and…"

"Puffins! They're so cute. I'd love to see them in the wild," Jess said. "Sorry, I interrupted."

"You've proved my point though. A cute bird or animal is more appealing than a lecture about littering. Those who see them might think twice about doing anything to harm them. I want to show where things are working well and encourage more of it."

"That's a wonderful idea," Jess said. "In the 'Before and After' ecology exhibition there were a couple of pieces where the after was the better one and it made me feel so positive."

"I'm glad you approve."

His words could have been patronising, but they weren't. He seemed pleased that she understood. She couldn't tell if that was just because his message was reaching people, or because he cared about her personal opinion.

The waiter brought their starters. Jessica ate her asparagus daintily, but without really tasting it. She consumed only the green tips, discarding the white portion. She tried to study Eliot without appearing to stare. The man had a healthy appetite and clearly enjoyed the sensual pleasure of good food.

Her father was the perfect host, ensuring he ordered wine which suited everyone's tastes and asking questions to keep the conversation flowing. Sometimes he could appear to show off, but that night he was relaxed. Perhaps because he knew he was with people who either loved him or who had good reason to be grateful for his generosity.

Jess was very careful not to drink too much and risk making a fool of herself. Even without a drink she wasn't sure she could stop herself trying to flirt with Eliot. When their main courses arrived, Jess picked at her salad, carefully avoiding every scrap of shredded white cabbage.

Eliot told a few entertaining stories about celebrities who'd wanted him to photograph them and then had temper tantrums when he explained he didn't photograph people.

"Naughty, as you do," Lizzie reminded him.

"Well yes, sometimes. They have to be interesting people though. People with more to them than just being temporarily famous."

"Quite right, boy."

"Because I've made a name for myself they think it'll do them good to have me take their portraits. It's as though they think I can use a special filter and add character in."

"It can be the other way round though, can't it?" Lizzie said.

"How do you mean?" Eliot asked.

"Jess, you must remember that horrible gossip magazine that wanted to do a piece on us when your father and I announced our engagement?"

"That was awful." She didn't know why Lizzie would want to bring that up. She'd been such a bitch about it.

"They had an agenda. They wanted to show us as a couple of spoilt little madams with nothing on our minds except designer labels and taking Aubrey for every penny we could get our greedy fingers on."

Well, they'd been right about one of them at least, Jess

reflected. Lizzie had got quite annoyed when it seemed she was about to be exposed.

"When we refused to be trailed on a succession of shopping trips to Harrods and jewellery stores they changed tack and tried to get us to fight so they could do the clichéd evil stepmother and mistreated daughter bit."

It was true, the reporter had pushed Jess into saying hurtful things to Lizzie, and the photographer, thanks to Jess, had managed to get unflattering pictures of Lizzie. Jess remembered asking her to see if any of Mum's jewellery needed cleaning or resetting and had then arranged it so the photographer got a picture of the new woman in Daddy's life apparently rifling his dead wife's jewellery box.

Jess started to speak and then stopped when she realised she had no idea what she wanted to say.

"They couldn't just accept us for what we really are," Lizzie finished.

Daddy had demanded the magazine cancel the article and delete all images and words, threatening to sue if anything was published without the written consent of both women. This was the first time the incident had been spoken of since. It was also the first time Jess clearly saw her own role in it. If she'd behaved with the same dignity as Lizzie it would never have got so bad. If she'd been willing to find out what Lizzie was really like instead of just believing every unflattering comment she'd ever heard, then it probably wouldn't have happened at all.

"Must have been pretty rotten for you," Eliot said to Lizzie.

"Worse for Jess," Lizzie said. "I'm used to being in the papers and having nasty things said about me because of my modelling, but she'd not come across this before and of course it was a difficult time for her."

Daddy nodded his head and looked as though he was getting ready to give his opinion on the cult of celebrity. Jess didn't want to hear it. She was just as bad as the people who read and produced the gossip magazines as she'd wanted to believe in an evil money-grabbing Lizzie who would soon be exposed. It was time she judged Lizzie on facts, not her own prejudice.

"Anyway, that's all over now," Jess said. "I'm sure Eliot won't be too disappointed that he's not going to be able to snap us having a cat fight."

"Not at all, I'm off duty."

Daddy beamed. "That's right, my two girls are wonderful friends."

Jess risked a glance at Lizzie and saw the other woman was looking at her to see how she'd taken that pronouncement. They both giggled.

"See what I mean?" Daddy asked.

Jess vowed she would try to make friends with Lizzie. Daddy would like it, which was important, but it would also be much easier and more pleasant for both of them.

The waiter brought their desserts. Jess almost gasped in horror when she saw her strawberries were covered in cream. She felt sick at the thought of the white cloying liquid coating the fruit she was expected to eat. As she stared at the glass dish it began to move away from her. Jess blinked and realised Lizzie was removing it. She scooped up the vanilla ice cream accompanying her chocolate torte, dropped it onto the cream covered fruit and passed the dark cake to Jess.

"Waiter messed up your order, Pumpkin? I'll call him back," Aubrey said and looked over his shoulder.

"No, Daddy, please I…"

"It's all right, we've just decided to swap," Lizzie told him.

"Women eh? Never know what they want, do they, boy?"

"In my experience they do and it's usually something they can't have," Eliot said.

Everyone laughed.

Under cover of her dad assuring Lizzie she could have whatever she wanted, Jess spoke quietly to Eliot.

"You're half right in my case," Jess said quietly. "I do know what I want."

Eliot raised an eyebrow in what might possibly be a suggestive manner. "And are you likely to get it, do you think?"

"I do and with your help."

He leaned close. "Tell me more." There was no doubt now that he considered her remark flirtatious and was happy to reciprocate.

"What are you two whispering about?" Aubrey asked.

"I was just telling Eliot that I too hope to be a photographer and thanking him for his advice about taking a course."

She glanced at Eliot. The surprise on his face suggested he'd only just made the connection with her and his email correspondent.

After dessert, Aubrey proposed a toast to happy partnerships. He was greeted by puzzled expressions.

"Oh, I didn't say, did I?"

The other three shook their heads.

"Eliot's inspired me. I've decided to fund a new clean-up project for a few acres at Dibden Spit. I got a letter about it. As it's just outside the New Forest it doesn't get looked after like a national park. The beach is covered in litter and is filthy due to pollution from an old factory. The land is covered with the car park and access roads and buildings which are no longer structurally sound. Druggies and the like hang about there now and it's a no-go area for local people. I'm going to have it cleared up and turned into a nature reserve. I'm told it's got good habitats for wading birds and rare butterflies and other things I've forgotten about. I'll employ local people to put in a visitor centre and run the place."

"That's wonderful, Daddy. When did you decide?" Jess asked.

She was speaking over Eliot who said, "Fantastic. That's exactly the kind of project I'm hoping to encourage."

Daddy beamed.

"Jess asked when you decided," Lizzie said. It seemed she too was wondering that.

"When I heard these two talking about photography saving the planet and that you agreed with them. The people who sent me that letter explained what could be done and everything, but it didn't seem like my sort of thing. I was just going to send some money. Dibden Spit is where you grew up, isn't it?"

Lizzie nodded. "I would like to see it cleaned up. As you say, it's been an eyesore and health hazard for a long time."

"Then Eliot told us about his new project. His pictures will help publicise what I'm going to be doing, get support from local people to really make it work. He'll get others interested too. Everyone likes good publicity, and with him involved there'll be masses of it. Other projects will start up. We can save the planet."

Daddy may have exaggerated a little, but it was hard not to get carried along with his enthusiasm. When he told other businessmen what he was doing, some of them would indeed be persuaded to follow his example.

"And it's the sort of thing you'd like to be involved in, isn't it, Pumpkin? Photography that makes a difference?"

"Oh yes!" She felt a rush of love for him. He'd understood when she'd tried to explain what she wanted to do.

"Then you shall. I'll fund Eliot's trip and an exhibition to show the results and then hire him to record the progress of my little efforts at Dibden Spit. I'll pay for whatever's needed to help spread the word."

"That's very generous, er, Aubrey. With your assistance, I'm sure it will be a great success." Eliot sounded cautious.

"Huh! With my money you mean. It's you and Jessica who will do the work and make it happen."

"Jessica?" Eliot asked at the same time as Jess said, "Me?"

"Yes, Pumpkin. You'll be going to Wales as Eliot's assistant."

Chapter 5

Jess was surprised, but delighted with the idea. Daddy wouldn't normally suggest she took a subordinate role. Doing so proved he understood her photographic ambitions and accepted her wish to become more independent from him.

Jess was aware of Eliot draining his glass. Judging by the whiteness of his knuckles grasping the stem, he wasn't enjoying a celebratory drink. The fact he'd gained a temporary assistant was clearly news to him. Unwelcome news.

Of course it was! Jess snapped out of her fantasy of a fortnight by Eliot's side. She'd suggested something similar and he'd said no. Jess had hoped to persuade him otherwise, but by earning a place with him, not have her father effectively buy it for her. Looking at Eliot's face, she was certain he wasn't for sale.

After a tense pause in the conversation, Eliot put down his glass, forced a smile and looked directly at Jess. "I'd be delighted to offer a few pointers, if you're seriously interested in photography. Perhaps when I get back you could bring me your portfolio and we can discuss what help you think I might provide?"

"Nonsense," Aubrey insisted. "Two weeks' master-class with you will be far better than a few pointers. Don't put yourself down, boy."

"Thank you, Eliot." Jess spoke loudly and clearly. "That

would be really useful." She hoped Daddy would let the matter drop. She didn't want to lose of the chance of help, or anything else, Eliot might offer.

"I'm not sure Jessica will enjoy this particular trip. I'll be travelling in a campervan…"

"I took a trip in a campervan once. Great fun it was. My chums and I actually slept and cooked in it. Can you imagine?"

Jess couldn't imagine her father doing any such thing, but was prevented from answering by Eliot saying that's exactly what he'd be doing. "Staying on location helps me get the best of the light. Even so, the trip will involve early starts and late finishes."

"Don't you worry about Pumpkin here. Tougher than she looks, you know. Now, let's hear no more about it, she's going."

"Aubrey, darling," Lizzie interrupted. "This has been quite a shock for Jessica and there's her college course to consider. Perhaps it will be best for her to show Eliot her portfolio, as he suggested, and for them to discuss the matter?"

"Hmm. I suppose I was getting a bit carried away. Come round tomorrow, Eliot, and tell us all about the trip. Pumpkin, you show him your pictures, see what he thinks and you decide if you want to go."

Jessica couldn't help being annoyed at how relieved Eliot looked. Was the thought of spending a fortnight with her really so awful?

"Will you be free tomorrow, Eliot?" she asked in an attempt to show she appreciated his offer of advice and wasn't trying to steamroller him into anything else.

His expression suggested her attempt was unsuccessful. "I'll give you a call, shall I?"

"That would be great. Thanks." Jess smiled brightly.

"Didn't you photograph Sonny Nova recently, Eliot?" Lizzie asked.

"Yes, I did."

"Oh, I like him," Aubrey said. "We met at a charity dinner a couple of weeks ago. Charming man, didn't you think?"

"Yes he is," Eliot agreed. "Funny too. One or two shots were unusable as I was shaking with laughter."

After that the mood lightened again and they enjoyed their coffee.

Jess stayed up late going through all her pictures to find the best. Most were of places in Old Portsmouth and Southsea as, since the photography module at college, she'd spent time in her local area putting into practice what she'd learned. For variety she included a few pieces of course work and some holiday shots. She left them out in order to make a final selection the following morning. She needed to get a decent amount of sleep – it wasn't just her photos she hoped to impress Eliot with. She hadn't been able to avoid noticing he wasn't overjoyed at Daddy's plan. She didn't want him forced into it, but if she could persuade him it was a good idea… The sight of him half naked, or rather half of him entirely naked, and then meeting him in person had already convinced her she'd enjoy spending two weeks in a confined space with him.

After a restless night, Jess spent longer choosing an outfit, styling her hair and applying make-up than she had to go out the previous evening.

He didn't ring on Saturday.

He didn't ring on Sunday.

Jess knew Eliot had her phone number; she'd given him one of her engraved cards. It was possible he'd lost it, but he knew Daddy's number too and her email address. Maybe he'd had an accident or was ill? There had to be some reason for his failure to call.

On Monday at college she repeatedly checked her phone. The other girls noticed and teased her.

"Didn't know you had a new boyfriend, Jess. Who is he?"

"I don't, this is just a man I met on Friday night." She didn't want to explain about Eliot not calling. For the same reason she'd kept away from Daddy and Lizzie. Often they all did something together at the weekend and Jess usually joined them for Sunday lunch. For the first time, instead of resenting Lizzie's constant presence by her father's side, she saw the other woman had every right to feel that way about Jess. If she did, Lizzie never showed it and always acted as though pleased to see her. In contrast, Jess often barely attempted to be polite.

Jess felt contrite at how she'd misjudged and treated Lizzie. However, it wasn't her only reason for giving them space. If Daddy learned Eliot hadn't phoned, he'd call him for her. That wasn't the answer. Jess wanted Eliot to want to call her, to want her.

She avoided looking at her phone when the others were about, but risked a glance when only Tanya was in sight.

"He must be someone pretty special," Tanya said.

"Why do you say that?"

"You've had dates before but I've never seen you checking your phone other than at lunchtime. Now you're obsessed."

"I've never had to check before; they've always called when I expected them to."

"And when were you expecting this guy to call?"

"Saturday morning."

"Jess, I don't want to sound mean, but if he said he'd call Saturday morning and he still hasn't, he's probably not that keen."

"He didn't actually say when, just that he'd call."

"That's not quite so bad, but…"

"He's still probably not that keen?"

"I'm afraid not. Who is he, Jess?"

"Eliot Beatty."

"The photographer?"

"Yep. And the model in that photo we saw. You remember the one?"

"Naked guy?"

Jess nodded.

"Wowzers! No wonder you're eager for him to call. What's the deal?"

Jess explained her father's plan for clearing up Dibden Spit and his idea she accompany Eliot to Wales as his assistant.

"Your dad has arranged for you to live in a campervan with a man you barely know?"

"No. For one thing we wouldn't actually be living in the van. It'll be a mobile studio. You know, like the trailers film stars have on locations so they can rest between shoots." As she said it Jess remembered what Eliot had said about staying on location. He probably did sleep in the van sometimes.

Tanya snorted. "That'd be right for you lot – buy a campervan and sleep in a hotel."

"I won't be doing either. He doesn't want me with him.

He's offered to give me some advice and I'm sure he'll keep his promise."

"Don't worry, if he wants your dad to fund his project then he'll call."

Tanya was right. Eliot called early that evening and said he could spare an hour the following day at the same time, if that would be convenient. His words were polite; the tone very much 'take it or leave it'.

Eliot arrived on time. He seemed rather taken aback by her apartment and something seemed to amuse him. Her father, and Lizzie, were already there, or she might have asked what that was.

Her dad again mentioned the clean-up project he was going to arrange, aided by the publicity from the pictures Eliot and Jess would take in Wales. He didn't actually say Eliot's taking Jess on the trip was a condition of the funding, but somehow seemed to imply it.

"Come on, Aubrey. Let's leave them to it," Lizzie suggested as soon as anyone, other than Daddy, could get a word in.

"Oh, righto."

It wasn't until he'd gone that it occurred to Jess she could have arranged to meet Eliot without telling her father. Why hadn't she done that?

"I'm sorry about how things went on Friday. I didn't know what my dad had in mind," she told Eliot.

He didn't look convinced. As she remembered telling him she knew what she wanted and planned to get it, Jess couldn't blame him. She tried to explain she'd accepted his emailed refusal and hadn't gone running to her dad to get him to persuade Eliot to agree to teaching her.

"So you don't want me to now?"

"I do, but…"

"But you're not prepared to do some actual work in return, let alone rough it in a campervan?"

"Yes! No. I really do want to be a photographer and I am prepared to work for that."

"I said I'd look through your work and try to offer advice, so why don't we do that?"

Jess handed him her portfolio.

Eliot slowly leafed through her folder of prints. He was proving he'd meant what he said, by doing what he'd offered. There was a way she could prove she hadn't wanted him manipulated into taking her on the trip.

"Eliot, if you decide you don't want to take me to Wales with you then I'll tell Daddy I don't want to go."

"You think you can convince him of that?"

"Yes." She couldn't convince herself that not going was the best thing and she definitely didn't want Eliot to feel that way. She could convince Daddy though. "And I'll make sure you get your funding too… Whatever happens."

She'd stick to that, if she had to, but she was going to do her best to persuade him to take her. Jess remembered the way Eliot and Lizzie had greeted each other. Clearly he was fond of her.

"I do want to come. I think it would be good for Dad and Lizzie to have some time alone together too. It must drive Lizzie mad that I'm always around, cramping their style."

"You don't need to go to Wales to stop doing that."

"Dad thinks of me as a child still and he's promised never to put anyone before me whilst I need him. That's why they haven't got married. This trip could be a first step in convincing him that I don't need protecting like that any more."

"Could it really?"

Jess thought for a moment that she'd made a mistake in confiding in him, but he went back to looking through the photos.

"Can I get you a drink?"

"Thanks. Tea if you've got it. Strong, splash of milk and two sugars."

"Coming right up!"

She brought in their drinks and a plate of biscuits, then tried to wait patiently for his reaction.

"They're in focus, that's a good start," he said. He gave her a lovely smile to show, she hoped, that this was a light-hearted remark, not the most positive thing he could think of to say.

"Why is this one in black and white?" Eliot asked, about a shot taken on Southsea Common on an exceptionally warm spring day.

"The people were all wearing different colours, some of them quite bright. I thought it distracted attention from what I wanted to show."

"Which was?"

"The spaces between them. See, every person or group of people seem to have exactly the same amount of space between them as though obeying some rule or even…"

"Go on."

"I was thinking of magnets. The people in each group pulled together and then repelled from the other groups, the way magnets are when turned around."

"You notice details, Jessica. That's important for a

photographer."

Of course it was. She couldn't photograph what she didn't see.

"And this one, tell me about this." Eliot indicated a gorgeous view she'd photographed on Capri. He was treating this as an audition or job interview. It wasn't. Eliot wouldn't pay any wages, in fact he'd gain financially by taking her. And he still didn't want her.

Jess tried to recapture the optimism and confidence she'd felt when on holiday with friends who believed she could do whatever she set her mind to. "I climbed a long way and wanted to capture the memory."

"I can't see your climb from this."

"Well no, it's what I saw when I got there, not me doing it. Surely you don't mean I should have taken it with my hiking boots in the frame?"

He laughed. "No, not quite. But perhaps if you'd pulled back a bit we'd have seen part of the path you took?"

"Actually, I took one of that to show how far I'd come. It's on the laptop."

"Let's see it, then."

She booted up her MacBook. Luckily she'd keyworded her holiday snaps and could quickly bring up the required image. "Here."

"Where is this in relation to the one you've printed?"

"It carries pretty much straight on," Jessica removed the pretty picture from the folder and held it above the computer screen.

"Now, if you'd framed it like this," he drew a rectangle in the air including the depth of both pictures but eliminating a couple of inches from both sides, "you'd show the view as well as the steep climb and you'd lose the waste-bin and sign."

"You're right." She could easily tell that his version of the shot would have been much better than hers.

"This one," he said, holding up the opened file. "What's your subject here?"

Surely that was obvious. The picture was of a lightning damaged oak tree which stood in the middle of a ploughed field. Other than the tree there'd been nothing else to look at, let alone worth photographing.

"The tree in the middle."

"Have you heard of the rule of thirds?"

Did he think she was an idiot? "Yes and look, the tree is only a third of the way up. I did it that way round because there was more interest in the sky than in the field." It was textbook stuff and she'd done it well. Her tutor had said so.

"OK, but you could have also put it to the left or right. That kind of arrangement is always more satisfying to look at, although I couldn't tell you why."

"Like having odd numbers of flowers in a vase?"

"Yes. And that field, it's not really dull is it? The pattern from the ploughing would make great lead in lines."

"Leading what?"

"What are they teaching you on this course you're doing?"

"Not much." She grinned. "I'd learn far more from you."

"Possibly." He gave a smile which made it clear he hadn't missed the inviting tone with which she'd delivered her last comment. "When I get back from Wales I'll arrange something."

"Unless I persuade you to take me."

"I'm not sure that would be such a great idea, Jessica."

"It would be such fun to go in a campervan; I've never even seen inside one. You could teach me so much. I can see you're right about the things you've said and I'm sure I could do much better."

"I'll be busy working, I won't have much time for that and we'll be fending for ourselves. It won't be what you're used to."

She noticed the 'we'. He was already imagining how they'd get on together. It wouldn't take much more to get him as enthusiastic as her. She wouldn't use Daddy's steamroller tactics though. Subtlety would do more good. Jess leant across him, allowing her hair to brush his arm and pointed out another photo. "What about this one?"

"The subject is good and you've composed the image quite well."

"But?"

He grinned. "That obvious, eh? You've taken it at the wrong time of day. Imagine long, dramatic shadows stretching across that path."

That would have looked better, but… "I can't photograph what isn't there."

"No, but you can put what you want into view."

"How?"

"You could have arrived earlier or stayed later."

"It was a college trip. Have you tried getting the average student out of bed early, or persuading them to continue studying when they needn't stay?"

"What about you, Jessica? Could you have stayed on and made your own way home, or returned early the next morning?"

She could, if it had occurred to her that would improve

the shot. Would she have done? Probably not; she'd been quite pleased with the result she'd obtained and seen no need to improve on it.

"Anyone can do what's easy. If you want to be better than average, you have to put in the effort."

"And I will when I know what to do." Even to her that sounded more defensive than convincing.

"You can take a reasonably competent photograph, Jessica. Why don't you stick with your college course? That'll get you a nice certificate and then you can go back to your privileged life and photograph friends' portraits for *Country Life* and produce their wedding albums. With your father's contacts I'm sure you'd do quite well."

She'd never been slapped, but imagined it would sting in just the way his words had. She wanted to slap back, but knew it would do no good. Jess doubted she'd win any kind of fight with him, mental or physical.

Eliot was watching her. Waiting for the reaction he surely knew he'd provoked.

Jess spoke as calmly as she could. "I want to be a good photographer. One who does the best she can and is valued for her skill more than her father's connections. Daddy's sweet and would do anything for me, but I want to do something for myself. I can't hide in his shadow forever."

"To be taken seriously you'll need to produce more than a few lucky shots. You'll have to get it right consistently. Can you do that, Jessica? Can you get a good shot when you're pressed for time, when the conditions are poor, you're tired and you're doing it because it matters?"

"Yes! At least, I can learn to."

"Why bother? You don't need to work."

"Not to live, no, but I have to do something with my time. I've pretty much wasted my life up to now because I didn't know what I wanted. Now I know. I want to be a photographer, a good one who makes people think, shows them things they might not want to see and forces them to do something about it. You mentioned me using Daddy's famous friends, well I can, not to bolster my ego, but to do some good."

"Nice speech, but will you still mean it on a cold morning after just a few hours' sleep?"

Tanya did good work at college despite getting little sleep and some older students on her course spent long hours in the pub and still made it to class the next morning. If they could cope then so could she. "As Daddy says, I'm tougher than I look."

Eliot still didn't look convinced.

She'd better get him back to training mode. "Which would have been better for this picture? Morning or evening? I suppose it would depend which way the shadows fell?"

"Partly that, but it's not just about the shadows. The light is too bright, too even. Have you heard of golden hour?"

"No."

"It's something it would be better to show you than explain."

"I hear the light is good in Wales."

He chuckled. "Persistent aren't you?"

"I get it from Daddy. I really do want to learn."

"I see you do."

"Well then," she invited. "Teach me."

"Wales won't be the best place for that. Like I said, I

really will be very busy. I'll hardly have time to look after myself, let alone worry about you."

"Great, so I can learn to work under pressure. I can help you too, carry things, maybe even massage your shoulders when things get tense."

"You can be quite persuasive."

"So you'll take me?"

"It's not a holiday, Jessica."

"I realise that."

"It's going to be long hours and hard work. You'd have to go where I said, when I said, usually on foot. You'd have to carry all your gear and some of mine. Cook and clean and cope with everything that living in the van involves."

"Deal." Did he say living in the van?

"Jessica! I didn't…" He dragged a hand through his hair. "Oh, come then, but you don't complain or whine. When you decide to quit I'll drop you at the nearest train station so you can come home to Daddy, and you stick to what you said about the funding for the Dibden Spit project."

"Fair enough. But I won't quit."

"We'll see."

Chapter 6

Once Eliot had left, Jess was tempted to phone Christina and her other friends to tell them about the trip to Wales. Christina's pretended jealousy and scandalous suggestions for how to fill time, whenever the light or weather prevented photography, would be lots of fun. Something she needed more than a good laugh was Zoe saying how lucky Eliot was to have her assistance and company, and Alyssa assuring her the whole thing wouldn't be a disaster. Jess was delighted Eliot had finally agreed, but aware he'd only done so reluctantly – and that she didn't know exactly what she'd talked herself into. Still, she'd be alone with Eliot; that was all that really mattered.

First though there was something more important she had to take care of; Daddy. He meant well, but…

As she climbed the stairs to his rooms, it occurred to Jess how she'd feel if Lizzie were to walk into her flat whenever she felt like it. Knocking on the door and waiting to be let into her childhood home would seem wrong, but she should make more effort to remember that Lizzie had as much right to be there as she did.

"Hello, Daddy, Lizzie?" she called out as she let herself in.

They both greeted her warmly.

"We've just opened a bottle of chardonnay," Lizzie said. "Can I tempt you to a glass, or would you prefer coffee?"

"Wine would be lovely. Thank you."

"We missed you this weekend, Pumpkin," her father said whilst Lizzie was in the kitchen.

"I didn't abandon you, Daddy, and it's only right that you and Lizzie have some time to yourselves, now you're engaged."

If it occurred to him that Jess had taken a long time to come round to that idea, he didn't say so. Usually whenever they talked about Lizzie, he would say something like, "You're my little girl and you'll always come first." In a way she couldn't blame him for the first part of that, as that's very much how she'd behaved; like a needy child who insisted on taking centre stage.

"So, has young Beatty seen sense yet?"

"He has agreed to take me with him. I'm going to speak to him in a few days to finalise the details." Actually, Eliot had said he'd give her a few days to realise what a bad idea it was and come to her senses, but it would help no one for her to say so.

"Finally! Don't know why he couldn't say so straight away. I had a good mind to ring him up and ask what he was playing at, but Lizzie said it might not be a good idea without speaking to you first."

Jess smiled at the other woman and not just because she was holding out a glass of wine. "She was right, Daddy. Thank you, Lizzie." She accepted the drink. "It would be best if I made the arrangements with him directly."

"There are a few things he…"

"Please, Daddy," she interrupted. "Let me do this myself."

"I was only going…"

"I know, but you're a very busy and important man. I'd hate to give you more work and now you've had the idea, all we have to do is see it through."

"Hmm." He glanced at Lizzie. "Are you two ganging up on me?"

"No, of course not, Daddy. Why would you think that?"

"Lizzie here said…"

"Aubrey darling," Lizzie squeezed his arm.

"What? Oh. Righto."

"Jess, I think your father mentioned that Dibden Spit is close to where I grew up?"

"Yes." Of course! Daddy was funding the clean-up for Lizzie, not just to help Jess's future career. Oddly, rather than being put out it wasn't all for her benefit, she felt a little relieved about that.

"I was wondering, hoping, that perhaps we could work together over this. Not the photography of course, but I would like to be involved."

Jess, unable to think of anything to say, just nodded.

"Maybe we can talk about it when you come back from Wales? I'm sure you've got plenty to think about and organise before then."

"Um, yeah. Good idea." Jess wasn't sure what she thought about teaming up with Lizzie and in just as much doubt as to what their involvement in the Dibden Spit project could be. She'd not thought about it other than as the means to persuade Eliot to take her to Wales and then another chance to spend time with him later on.

"Thank you, Jess."

"My two girls working together? What a team you'll make!"

Jess raised her wine glass and clinked it against Lizzie's.

Her father offered to have his PA make Jess's hotel bookings and to pay for any new equipment she might want. Jess refused both, explaining the weather would dictate where they would be and when, so advanced booking would be impossible and that she didn't yet know if there was anything else she would need to buy. "But if there is, I'm sure my allowance will cover it."

When, half an hour later, Jess had finished her wine and let herself out, she heard her father say, "There's something different about my little Pumpkin. Do you think she's all right?"

"Yes, Aubrey. I think she's starting to grow up."

If Lizzie had heard the giggling Skype chat with Zoe, Alyssa and Christina about living with Eliot for a couple of weeks, she might have changed her mind about that. Or maybe not; some of Christina's advice was decidedly 'adult'.

Jess tried not to fantasise about the trip, but found she was thinking of little else. She wasn't sure if Eliot really meant they'd be living in the van, or had just been trying to put her off, but she could see it was a possibility. Having the campervan parked on location wouldn't help him get the early morning light if he was sleeping in a hotel in town. Leaving the location to come and collect her would waste even more time, so her staying somewhere more comfortable on her own wasn't an option. At least not for the entire time as she really did intend to learn all she could, including how to benefit from the early morning 'golden hour'.

Jess wasn't about to ask Eliot if he'd been bluffing, so instead rang to ask what she should bring with her.

"As little as possible. There's not much storage, so a sleeping bag in a compression sac will be better than a quilt."

That confirmed it, they'd definitely be sleeping in the same small space for part of the time.

"How many people does the van sleep?" she asked.

"Three in theory. Why?"

"I'm just wondering how big it is."

"It isn't big at all, which is why I don't want to take anything which isn't absolutely necessary."

Like her. She was sure that's what he meant; she could hear the irritation in his voice.

"You'll want all your camera gear, obviously, but go easy on everything else. Power is an issue, so no hair straighteners or anything daft like that."

Jess resisted explaining they'd actually save space. Without them her hair became a mass of springy curls which filled a considerable area. She had the feeling he might order her to have it cut short and she absolutely wasn't going to do that.

What did she want to bring that he couldn't object to? "How about my laptop?"

"Of course."

She tried to tell him how much she was looking forward to the trip, but he seemed exasperated by her chatter and reminded her the primary reason for it was so he could do his job.

"I know that and I'll help, not just get in the way."

"I'm trying to work now."

"Shall I ring back at a more convenient time?"

"I'll be very busy until we go, so there won't be a convenient time. I'll email you the details."

Jess tried not to take it personally, after all he didn't

really know her. Once he saw how helpful she could be, and how much fun to have around, he'd be sorry for his reluctance to take her and generally being so negative.

She didn't have long to wait for his emailed instructions.

Jessica,

I'll pick you up at 10.30 21st May. Please be ready to leave. I'll be returning on 1st June. You, of course, are welcome to make your own way home at any time before that. You need to bring enough practical clothing for however long you'll be with me or be prepared to use a public launderette, if we can spare the time to find one.

There's no mains electric, but there will be the opportunity to charge some equipment. Priority will be given to my camera equipment and laptop, then yours. After that my phone, then yours. If anything else needs power, don't bring it. Phone and internet signal won't be good.

I'll get in some food for the first few days. Do you have any allergies or anything?

Please sign and return attached contract.

Eliot.

She hadn't been expecting him to sign off with love and kisses, but that seemed extremely brusque. She tried to believe he simply was really busy and hadn't time to give her more than the most basic facts.

Jess didn't want to annoy him further by wasting time or seeming difficult. He'd said she'd be cooking, so she should have some control over what she ate. She'd take along a sachet of saffron and a few colourful, zesty sauces in case his tastes were too bland for her.

She considered asking Daddy to get his legal team to

check the contract, but that would cause a delay and probably complicate matters. The document was written in plain English and simply to clarify that she would retain copyright of any images she took under his direction during the trip, but that she consented to his use of any of them in the planned exhibition. If used, they would be credited to her. That seemed fair, so she signed it electronically and attached it to her reply.

Hi Eliot.

Thanks, that's all very clear.

I don't have any food allergies. It was good of you to think of my food preferences. Please can any rice, bread or pasta be wholemeal? Other than that, I eat most things.

I'm really looking forward to learning a lot and proving to you that I can work hard and that having me along is a good thing!

See you soon,

Jess.

She entered the dates into her diary and realised that instead of the fortnight she'd been expecting, it was only twelve days, two of which would involve travelling for several hours. Had he deliberately shortened the trip to reduce the amount of time he'd be spending with her? No, it was more likely he'd not been precise when he first mentioned it, or maybe he'd realised that with her help he could work much faster.

Jess wasn't sure if Eliot had been exaggerating about the lack of phone signal, but in case he wasn't she warned Daddy and her friends she probably wouldn't be in touch very often and might not receive their messages. She promised to tell them all about the trip on her return. It was a little disconcerting that she might not be able to easily communicate with anyone but Eliot for the next twelve days, but oddly freeing too. That was until she realised communication with Eliot might be harder than trying to connect to the internet in some deep, dark and remote Welsh valley.

She visited a camping shop to choose a sleeping bag and a selection of practical clothing. Jess also considered buying proper climbing boots, but after discussing it with the sales assistant agreed there wouldn't be time to wear them in and reluctantly decided her old hiking ones would have to do.

"It might be a good idea to re-waterproof them if you haven't done that already," he said.

Jess admitted her 'old' boots had been bought less than three months previously. Other than a few walks along the beach at Southsea to get used to them, one sightseeing stroll on Capri and a couple of photography excursions, they hadn't been worn.

The assistant put down the waterproof spray and pointed out a range of anti-blister socks. Jess bought every pair in her size.

Her only other purchases were two strong canvas bags to put everything in. As they could be folded up, they'd be easier to stow in a confined space than her Louis Vuitton suitcases. Once she'd added the bare minimum of toiletries, and enough underwear to last the trip, the bags were almost full. Pyjamas needed more space than filmy negligees, but she packed them anyway. She wasn't Christina and, whatever Jess's intentions, she and Eliot weren't yet even good friends. That was going to change in Wales, but there was no need to rush into anything else.

As Jess passed the computer shop, she remembered telling Tanya about a new lens being only slightly better than the one she already owned and how the other girl had reacted to her extravagance and insensitivity. She'd had a point on that occasion, but this was different. Jess's laptop was over a year old and the newer model boasted a considerably longer battery life. If power was an issue in the campervan that would be useful; she couldn't do anything with her photos on a dead computer.

When she got her new laptop home, Jess transferred everything over and deleted the memory of the old one. She put it back in its box, wrapped it and took it to college on her last day, along with chocolates for everyone to share. Her classmates presented her with a huge leaving card which they'd all signed and a massive box of chocolates. They were the same brand and size as the ones Jess had brought. It had taken until her last day, but she had learned to fit in with the others.

Once the chocolates were gone, which didn't take long, Jess just wanted to give Tanya the laptop and go, not get involved in any emotional goodbyes. She scribbled a note saying, *Please meet me in the coffee shop at 12 I have...* She nearly finished it 'something for you' but changed it to 'a favour to ask'. Tanya might decide to refuse a gift, but Jess didn't think she'd be able to resist seeing what Jess could want from her.

She was right. When Tanya arrived she saw the gift-wrapped box and said, "You'd better not have bought anything for me."

"I haven't."

"So you really do have a favour to ask?"

"Yes. You know how I don't have a clue what it's like to be a normal person, the kind who has to work for a living?"

"Yep. Look, if you haven't bought me a present and

really want a favour, I'm going to let you buy me something to eat to make up for the lunch I'm missing in the canteen."

Jess grinned. "That's decent of you! OK, deal."

Tanya picked up a menu. "Go on, I'm listening."

"Eliot has agreed to take me to South Wales, but he's made it very clear that I'll be working, not taking a holiday. To be honest, what you said about him only agreeing because my dad is funding a project which he's keen on, is right. I think he feels as though he's been cornered into taking me and resents that."

Tanya nodded. "Yeah, probably."

"You were right about us living in the van too."

"Aha."

"Thing is, I know I can be annoying. I really like him and I really do want to learn, but I don't want twelve days of hell. Can you give me any tips on being… Well, not being like you thought I was?"

"I can try. Let's order and I'll think while we wait."

Tanya opted for a Brie and bacon baguette. Jess chose smoked salmon on dark rye. They both ordered coffee and chocolate brownies. Tanya asked for ice cream on hers. "As you're paying." She left Jess at the till and went in search of a table.

"Can you put extra ice cream and flakes and sauce and stuff on her brownie?"

"Sure. How much do you want?"

"Five pounds worth?"

"No problem."

When they'd eaten their sandwiches, Tanya said, "I think that remembering it's work and treating the trip like a job you need to keep to pay the rent might help. OK, forget the rent – but a job you want to keep."

"Makes sense."

"You worked before you started college, didn't you?"

"Yes. I was my father's PA."

"Ah. So you didn't have to put up with much grief?"

"No. None." She'd not had much work or responsibility either as he'd kept on his existing PA too. That had been frustrating for Jess, but not in the way Tanya meant.

Tanya was quiet for a few moments, then said, "I'm guessing you have a cleaner?"

"Yes."

"Right, remember I'm trying to help and not having a go?"

"OK."

"This cleaner, is she always smiling and polite and acts like she doesn't mind picking up after a spoiled little rich kid who can't be bothered to keep her place tidy?"

"When I see her, yes, Mrs Jennings is always cheerful."

"Do you think she ever has a bad day, or wishes she was somewhere else or doing something else?"

"She must do, I suppose." Jess always asked after Mrs Jennings' family and remembered her birthday, but never thought how the woman might feel. Very possibly she wasn't always as happy as she seemed.

"Be like her. Act like you're happy to be doing whatever he wants you to do. Within reason, obviously. If you spill stuff on your floor Mrs Jennings has to act like it's no problem to clean it up, even if it's something gross. If you have people round, she has to pretend she isn't annoyed to have extra work on the day she was hoping to finish early. If you mention you can't find something she has to help you look and act like she doesn't realise you're accusing her of nicking it and if it doesn't turn up she'll never get another job."

"Tanya, I…"

"Sorry, got carried away. Mum cleans in an estate agent's office. Someone heard her ring tone and because it was the same as the one on the phone they'd lost, they thought she'd pinched it. It wasn't even the same make, but if the rumour had got to the agency she'd have been out of work. Mum's had to clear up after Christmas parties and when a customer's dog was sick, which meant staying late even though she's got a baby to get back to."

"That's awful!"

"No, it isn't, Jess. That's having a job in the real world. Sometimes they're lovely to her. If there's a big sale they leave her a piece of the cake they bought to celebrate and she gets invited to the parties she has to clean up after. More than that though, it means we all have somewhere to live and food to eat."

As she said the last bit, the waitress appeared with their brownies. Jess's was a neat square of cake on a small white plate. Tanya's had so much ice cream, whipped cream, chocolate buttons and sauce that it was spilling over the edge of the huge bowl. "Sorry, no flakes," the waitress said as she left a generous supply of serviettes, which Tanya would probably need.

"Jess!"

"We can swap if you don't want it." She reached towards the bowl.

"Get off!" Tanya, rashly, stuck a spoon into the gooey mess and narrowly missed sending the ice cream into her lap.

As they ate their dessert, Jess thought about Tanya's advice. Eliot said she'd have to get up early, help with carrying things, cook, and tidy the van. She might not always want to, but that was part of the deal, so she'd have to smile and get on with it. "Yes, I see. And your mum's boss think she's always cheerful and they ask after her baby, not realising she'd rather go straight home to her than stay and chat."

"Something like that."

"Thanks. I think that will help. OK, another question about normal people. I know you need a new laptop, but you can't afford one yet."

"Tell me about it."

"Suppose someone offered you a second-hand one, which they didn't need and was better than the one you've got now. Would you see that as patronising and be offended?"

Tanya looked again at the gift-wrapped box Jess had placed on a spare chair. "Are you kidding me?"

"I needed to get one with a longer battery life." She placed the old one in front of Tanya. "Please take it."

"Have you already bought the new one?"

"Yes and transferred everything over. You'll need to upload any programs you need, but I think you can get them at a student rate, so hopefully the money you've saved will cover that."

"It will. Thanks, Jess." There was a wobble in Tanya's voice and her eyes looked incredibly shiny.

"Look, I have to go now. Say goodbye to everyone for me, will you?" She was gone before Tanya could reply.

Chapter 7

Jess squeezed a few cooking ingredients as well as her toiletries, wallet, phone and laptop into the smaller of the two new canvas bags she'd bought to hold her clothes. Her cameras and lenses went into a strong, lockable waterproof case. That would keep them safe whilst travelling, but was too heavy and unwieldy to carry anywhere so she was also taking a backpack, specially designed for photographers, for everyday use.

She left her empty backpack, camera case and one bag of clothes ready by the door and carried everything else down to meet Eliot, who'd arrived exactly on time. The campervan wasn't white as she'd expected, but silver-grey and about the size of a supermarket delivery van.

"Hi," she called as she jogged over to him. "Looks like we're going to have good weather."

Eliot didn't return her smile. "Ready?"

"Yes."

"You're not if that's your idea of sensible footwear."

She was wearing comfortable and practical, yet pretty, flat leather sandals. "What's wrong with these?"

"You can't climb mountains or cross boggy ground in them."

Did he seriously think a girl would go away for almost a fortnight with only one pair of shoes? "I have hiking boots and flip-flops."

He didn't respond, just jumped out and opened a door at the rear, revealing a storage area, roughly half the height of the interior. Guessing that's where she was supposed to put her gear, Jess stepped around Eliot to put her bag on the floor of the van. He still said nothing.

"Eliot, I know you don't really want me coming with you and feel you've been manipulated into taking me."

"With good reason."

"OK, yes. But you have agreed to it. This is happening. How about we at least try to get along?" She offered her hand.

He shrugged, then clasped her hand. "I suppose I'd been thinking of you as a little girl who'll just get in the way."

"I'm not so little," Jess said, sticking out her chest in what she hoped was a jokey manner.

He gestured to her bag. "Have you got anything else?"

"Yes." She wasn't going to apologise. He must realise she had, as he'd told her to bring all of her camera equipment.

"I'd better give you a hand."

"Thank you so much." She returned to her own rooms to fetch a pot of basil. "Can we take this?" When she saw his expression, she explained, "It's to eat, not for decoration."

"Does it taste nice?"

"It's fab on pasta, I promise."

"I suppose it can sit in the sink." Eliot picked up her case, as though it only weighed half what it really did. "Sure you've got everything? You don't need any medication or anything that you've forgotten?"

"It's all here." She tapped the bag which contained a selection of sauces and spices as well as her toiletries and other personal items.

"OK. Keep anything you might want quickly in there. You'll find that getting to anything in the back, in the middle of the night when it's raining isn't convenient."

"Right. I'll try to remember."

"It's a long drive, I'd rather get going now than wait until you've put all your stuff away. That OK with you?"

"Yes, fine."

Eliot put her case in the back of the van, shuffling things round a bit so it was securely wedged in and then took her clothing bag and backpack from her and placed them on top of both their camera cases. He slammed the rear doors shut.

"Come on then, I'll give you the grand tour and a last chance to change your mind." He pulled open a sliding door at the side of the van and reached inside to flick a switch. Immediately a small step slid out from under the door sill. He jumped in ahead of her and opened doors to reveal well filled cupboards.

Jess looked in from outside and smiled at the pale wood effect floor and trim, the neat storage solutions and the turquoise cushions. It was obvious why Eliot had been surprised by her rooms when he'd first gone there. The van was very much a miniature version of her apartment. It was much nicer than she'd expected. Much smaller too.

"The seats at the front swivel round to face the table when I want them to. This table can be fixed to the side of the van outside if we want to eat al fresco."

"I'm not a big fan of eating standing up," she said without thinking. Why pick holes when he was telling her the advantages of what seemed to be his pride and joy?

"Me neither, but I've packed folding chairs. This is the

kitchen." He indicated two gas burners and a dinky sink. "Fridge." He opened the door, showing it was crammed full of food. "Bathroom." He slid open an internal door.

Jess stepped up into the van to take a closer look.

"The toilet flushes, there's a sink and shower."

"Pretty good."

"I'll have to show you how to use them, but it's not difficult. And this is obviously the bedroom."

At the rear of the van was a double bed complete with duvet and pillows, all in the same turquoise as her own bedlinen. She realised the bed was raised up to create the storage space which now contained her clothes and camera equipment.

"A double bed?"

"Yes, proper mattress too. Oh, don't worry, the bench seat and table at the front convert into a single. I'll be having the double. Where you sleep is up to you."

She wanted to give him a disapproving look, but wasn't quite sure she could manage it, so opened one of the cupboards under the sink instead. Inside were proper china plates, cups and real glasses all stacked in racks.

"The van's lovely, Eliot. I'm really looking forward to living here for a while."

"It'll look less pretty when it's full of wet clothes and muddy boots and it's your turn to empty the toilet cartridge."

"I'll have to…?"

"Yes you will. It's not difficult and I've got rubber gloves." He chuckled. "This trip is going to be an all-round education for you."

Jess tried to match his smile. Emptying the toilet couldn't be worse than some of the things she'd done for

Mum in those last weeks. "I'm perfectly willing to take my turn with all the work, once you've shown me how."

He nodded. "I believe you think you are at any rate."

"I think it's going to be a lot of fun." She gave a warm smile.

"If you say so. Are we ready? I rather expected your father to appear for a big send off."

"Ah, well he doesn't think you're coming until two. I've left a note to say we'd got away earlier than planned."

"Did you now?" For the first time he smiled. "Then I suppose we'd better make our getaway before he arrives."

Jess put her bag on the bench, which was the opposite side of the small table behind the driver's seat.

Eliot shook his head. "Put it on the floor."

After she'd moved it he added, "That's better. It can't fall from there."

He was right, she did have a lot to learn. Already she had the feeling that photography might be the easy part.

They'd been travelling, without speaking much, for a couple of hours when Jess's stomach rumbled loudly. She'd been too keyed up for breakfast and it was past noon – the time she'd got used to having lunch at college.

"Hungry?" he asked.

"Famished."

"There's a coffee shop at the next service station. That do you?"

"Perfect."

He held the door open for her as though such ordinary politeness was a big deal. When he asked what she'd like to eat and where she wanted to sit, he made it seem as though she'd demanded they take a break, rather than simply agreed with his suggestion.

Eliot refused Jess's attempt to pay for their coffee, pizza slices and cakes.

"I'll get it next time then," she said.

"Unless you're on the train home by then."

"Not going to happen."

He grinned at that and nodded as though conceding defeat.

"Do you need a special licence to drive a campervan?" Jess asked.

"Not one this size. Why?"

"I could share the driving."

"No."

"I said I'd help, but I can't do that if you won't let me."

"It's not insured for anyone but me to drive."

Jess considered offering to get herself insured, but Daddy had paid for her policy and she didn't have any of the details with her. If she hoped to impress Eliot she had to do something which didn't involve contacting her father and persuading him to pay out.

They drank their coffee in silence for a few minutes, then he asked about her college course, wondering if taking time off would prove a disadvantage.

Jess explained that she'd left. "I've already completed the stills photography module anyway. The rest doesn't particularly appeal to me."

"Why did you take that course then?"

"You suggested I do something general and it seemed to be the best bet available with my qualifications. I gave up sixth form when Mum became ill and then sort of drifted into working for Daddy after…" She took a deep breath and another sip of coffee. "It was OK for a while, but I can't do that for the rest of my life. I want something that's all me, not just Daddy's little girl. Does that make sense?"

"I think so. Your father no doubt has good points, but he's a bit overpowering."

"He is."

"So you've settled on photography, or is that just something you're trying out?"

"It really is what I want to do." She'd told him that already, and doubted he'd forgotten. "You think I'm just playing at this, wasting your time?"

"The thought had crossed my mind."

"I'm not. I've seen how good photography can be at getting messages across. I want to be able to communicate, make a difference."

"Hmm, OK but professional photography is a competitive business. You'll be up against skilled professionals as well as every amateur who owns a digital camera and has grasped the basics of Photoshop."

"Good thing I'm learning from the best then."

"Flattery will get you almost anywhere."

"Today I'm hoping it will get me to South Wales."

"We'd better get going. In order to save a bit of fuel, I didn't fill up with water before I left home, so I'll get some now. Maybe you'd like to sort out your clothes and things while I do that?" He parked the van close to the water supply and took a large plastic container from the back, leaving the doors open for Jess to get to her clothes.

"I've kept one overhead locker empty for you. If you need more space than that, just put stuff wherever you can, or leave it in the back."

She stowed her clothes in the lockers over the bed and put her washbag in the bathroom. It was when she was doing that she spotted neatly folded turquoise towels. She was so used to them being provided in hotels whenever she travelled anywhere that she hadn't considered bringing some and in any case, there wasn't room for more. She hoped Eliot wouldn't mind sharing.

Jess grabbed the chance to text her father and let him know they were part way to Wales and everything was fine. Then she fired off a few quick notes to her friends. She was giggling over Christina's response to the fact his double quilt was the same colour as the one in her flat, when Eliot opened the van door.

"You'd better use the toilets." He gestured to the public toilets attached to the coffee shop.

She'd realised he'd be telling her what to do most of the trip, and thanks to Tanya was prepared to try to accept that. But this was overdoing it – and just a bit weird.

"I'm OK, thanks."

"We have to use public toilets whenever we can, Jessica," he warned her. "The van doesn't carry much water so we don't want to waste it flushing when we don't need to, and of course if the toilet is filled up it will have to be emptied…"

"By me. Right, I see."

The next part of the journey was much more pleasant. Eliot explained what he hoped they'd achieve during the trip, both the photographs he'd previously intended to take and the extra ones to be used in the exhibition Aubrey Borlase had promised to fund.

"He intended that to help, not create more work. I suppose he thought you could do both together." Jess tried not to sound too defensive of her father, without belittling the increased workload Eliot was faced with.

"I probably can in a lot of cases, but I don't want to use the same images more than once. They lose impact if seen repeatedly."

"I know what you mean," Jess said. "I get fed up with seeing the same short news clips being used over and over when there must be far more footage available. It makes it seem staged or unreal somehow."

"Or TV and film trailers. Basically they're saying that's the only good bit."

"They're usually right! So, you'll be taking different sets of photos at once?"

"When I can. I'm working for people with slightly different agendas as well as capturing stock images, so there's scope for that."

At college Jess had learned about uploading photographs to stock libraries where the photographer earned commission on sales. She wasn't ready for that yet and probably Eliot no longer had to, as his reputation meant people would buy directly from him. Naturally there was a big difference in the marketability of their work, but she'd soon be a little nearer to his level. Of more importance was the fact she understood him and they felt the same way about a lot of things. It wasn't just their skill levels which would become much closer during the trip.

When they neared the Severn crossing, Eliot asked her to take £6.70 from the pot which was set in the dashboard. As she placed the coins in his hand and felt the warmth of his skin, Jess couldn't help looking forward to the enforced intimacy of the next few days.

Guessing Eliot would prefer to keep the conversation more practical, she asked, "Will we be based at one location, or moving around?"

"Most of the time we'll be based near St Brides, but as I've organised shoots at the National Trust's Stackpole and Southwood estates and another up at Porthgain, we'll spend some nights away."

"So you're working for the National Trust?"

"They'll be using some of the images and they've given permission for shoots, but it's not just about one particular organisation. Girl Guides cleaned one beach. In another place the local community all got together to make a small stretch of coastline safe. The local paper covered that. Absolutely everyone got involved, even octogenarians were down there litter picking, making cups of tea and serving up cake. Now the coastal path is safe for anyone to use. Locals don't really use it much, so it wasn't a self-help thing. If they hadn't done it the council were going to close the whole path claiming there weren't the resources and manpower to get it fixed. The bill for the scaffolding and signs and the rest to close it was going to cost more than three times what it cost to fix the problem, but the money for that… Oh, sorry, I've gone into lecture mode."

"That's OK, it's obviously something you care about. I think I understand. People see the difficulties rather than getting things done?"

"Yes, and doing nothing can cost more in the end, not always in money. Still, that's not what this trip is about. I want to show what can be done, has been done and try to encourage others to do the same. All the images will be positive, show beautiful scenery, dramatic landscapes, cute wildlife, stuff like that. My exhibitions are free to view, so I get lots of people wandering in off the streets just because it happens to be raining or they missed a bus and so had a few minutes to spare. They don't want to be lectured to, but I do want to reach them."

"A bit like your 'Before and After' exhibition?"

"A bit, but I want to show things in a different way. Not be so obvious."

"Right."

"You sound sceptical."

"I'm sure you could do it, but will people understand your message?"

"You don't think so?"

"My friend Tanya and I tried really hard to understand what you were showing and discussed them all afternoon. We weren't always sure and we were studying that kind of thing. I'm not saying we're particularly bright or that the course is any good, but I don't suppose the average member of the public, who just wanders around for a quick look because it happens to be raining, is much more likely to understand?"

"I suppose you're right."

"Wow!" Jess said as they turned a corner and caught sight of a valley below them.

"That's what I meant about the light." He pulled into a lay-by. "At the start and end of the day it has this warm kind of glow to it. Golden hour it's called, although you can't rely on anything like sixty minutes' worth. Get the light right, catch the perfect moment and you can make a good picture out of almost anything. With the right subject, just one look is enough to take your breath away."

She turned to see the way the light sparkled in his eyes. The warm glow of sunlight stroked his face and made her think of him lying on her bed at home with the morning sun playing over his naked body. She'd had that fantasy so many times it almost seemed like a memory.

His smile suggested he would like to give her something to remember.

No, she shook her head. She was seeing what she wanted to. With reluctance, Jess dragged her thoughts and the conversation back to landscape photography. "This view would be stunning anyway, surely?"

"Maybe 'nice' but not 'wow'."

"Are we going to photograph it?"

"We can stop if you like, but that'll mean we arrive in the dark and you'll be cooking my dinner late."

"That's OK." Then, when she noticed his raised eyebrow and remembered Tanya's advice, added, "I mean it's OK with me if you don't mind the delay."

He grinned. "Come on then."

They both climbed out. Eliot grabbed a backpack and waited as Jess selected a camera and lens from her case.

"It would be helpful if you kept the equipment you'll use most often, ready in your backpack. That way, we can make the most of any unexpected opportunities."

"Yes, I…" She just stopped herself saying that's why she'd brought it. "Think that's a good idea."

They both took several photographs. Eliot returned to the van to fetch a tripod.

"Why are you using that?"

"I'll show you later."

"That's not fair!"

"You can borrow it if you like."

"I didn't mean that. I want to know what you're doing. I'm here to learn."

"To learn to copy me, or to think for yourself?"

"Oh all right." She knew she sounded petulant. If Eliot

noticed then it simply amused him.

"Photograph anything you like. Just try stuff and this evening we'll see what worked and what didn't."

Jess, encouraged by this suggestion, took lots of shots. Some using a wide angle lens to photograph the whole valley, some close ups on small rock formations or long shots of where the last of the light was reflected in a lake at the bottom.

She was looking forward to seeing how they turned out and to seeing Eliot's images of this beautiful place. She was also looking forward to a cosy night in with him, but she tried to keep her thoughts professional.

"Enough?" Eliot asked as the light faded.

"Yes, I don't think we'll get anything more here this evening."

"I agree."

It was only then she realised she'd continued photographing long after he'd stopped. "Sorry, did I take too long?"

"I expect you'll get the answer to that when you look at the results."

"Right. I wondered if I was holding you up or anything."

"I would have said."

She believed him and hurried to put her camera gear back in the van so he wouldn't be tempted to do just that.

They drove until Eliot said they were close to where they were staying for the night. "There are directions in the glove box."

Jess opened it and found a sheet of handwritten instructions.

"The chap who owns the field where we'll be staying

said not to use the sat-nav once we were through the town as there's a bit of a problem with it in this area."

Jess did her best to navigate for him, but the writing wasn't that easy to read and in the gloom of the evening the road signs were almost impossible to see. When they reached what seemed to be their destination she asked, "Are you sure we're in the right place?"

"You're the navigator."

"There's nothing here."

"I did say we'd be roughing it, so don't start complaining there's no spa and five star restaurant on site."

"I didn't mean that."

"Oh?"

She wasn't sure what she had meant really. Parking in a field wasn't what she'd imagined, but then she hadn't known what to expect.

"I see why you warned me about lack of wifi," she said, trying to sound cheerfully accepting.

"Not a chance here, but sometimes there's a mobile signal."

Jess guessed her attempts to look happy with the situation were more successful as she recalled Christina's comments about providing their own entertainment.

"Come on," Eliot said. "I'll show you how to get everything going."

Jess reached to unclip her seat belt and found Eliot's hand in hers. The touch was almost certainly accidental, but not unwelcome to Jess. At least, not until she realised that twelve days spent so close to this gorgeous man might be more frustrating than fun.

Chapter 8

"This lever is to release your seat, so you can turn it round," Eliot said.

"Right." Of course he'd just meant the practicalities of using the van. That was a good thing; although attracted to him she didn't want a casual fling and it didn't seem he wanted any kind of relationship with her at all. Perhaps not even the professional one which, she reminded herself, was her main reason for being there.

Eliot showed Jess how to switch on the gas, operate the water heater, cooking equipment and bathroom facilities and how to close everything down again ready to move off. "I'll close the blinds and you can start dinner."

Jess looked through the fridge and cupboards and selected ingredients for spaghetti bolognese and a salad. There was a jar of sauce to make it from, and plenty of wholemeal spaghetti, so it wouldn't be a problem and presumably it was something he liked.

"What we having?"

"Spag bol."

"Great. There's a bottle of red in there." He indicated the cupboard where the plates were. "Want me to download your pictures?"

She wasn't keen on him seeing them before she had, but couldn't use the computer and cook at the same time, and he'd be seeing them soon anyway. Besides, there wasn't much room on the table for two laptops. "Sure."

Just as she would at home, Jess started assembling everything she'd need to make dinner. She immediately realised cooking in the van was going to be awkward, even for someone as obsessively tidy as her. There was no workspace other than the small table they'd eat from and which Eliot was currently using half of. Soon that was full of the ingredients she'd removed from the fridge. She added the wine bottle and two glasses and took the plates from the rack. Eliot didn't look up but perhaps sensed she was there holding them. He swivelled his chair half-way back to the driving position, placing the laptop on his thighs and his feet up on the seat Jess had used for the journey down. Apparently giving her as much space as possible was going to be his only contribution towards preparing dinner.

Jess took a deep breath and reminded herself cooking was part of her job and it was a job she wanted to keep. She exhaled slowly, then opened the wine to let that breathe.

Eliot poured wine into both glasses. She almost laughed at his doing that just after she'd thought he'd expect to be waited on.

"Cheers," he said and raised his glass.

Jess tapped hers against it. "To a good trip?"

"Indeed." There was a twinkle in his eye suggesting that he was thinking of something more than photography. Or was she imagining that?

Jess put down her glass ready to peel an onion and sent the corkscrew clattering onto the floor. The plates she'd got out had to be put back so she had somewhere to use the chopping board. The basil plant got watered whenever she rinsed anything, as there was nowhere for it to go other than its travelling home of the sink. Progress was slow, but Jess congratulated herself on coping brilliantly.

They sipped their drinks as she cooked and he tapped away at the keyboard. It was companionable to be so close to the man as she prepared his meal. She'd be close to him as they slept tonight, too. There was less than ten feet between the double bed where Eliot would be and the bench seat which would make Jess's bed. She tried to keep her thoughts on the present.

Jess served up their food. Eliot switched off the computer and swivelled his seat back round. Jess sat opposite. They ate the meal with all but one light switched off. It was cosier than the most romantic of restaurants.

After they'd eaten, Eliot washed up at the tiny sink. The basil plant didn't cause him a problem as he simply put it on the floor between his feet. Jess dried and put everything away, and was pleased she'd remembered where most things went.

As soon as he'd emptied the washing-up bowl, Eliot replaced the basil plant and returned to working on his computer. When everything else was safely back in its place, Jess sat back on the bench seat. Eliot placed his laptop next to her and slid in beside her. He pressed a key to show a slideshow of the best images they'd taken earlier.

The first few were as breathtaking as she remembered that first glimpse of the valley, they had to be Eliot's. Then came a detail of sun glistening on a wet rock.

"Oh, is that mine?"

"Can't you tell?"

"I thought it might be, but I'm not sure."

"You don't see the picture in your mind before you take it?"

"No. You do?"

"Hmmm. Now here's the one I used the tripod for." He showed her an image of the valley.

Instead of positioning himself, as Jess had done, to reduce the appearance of the road, he'd made a feature of it. The picture was framed so that as the road snaked from side to side, it touched the edges. That accentuated the bends and curves. What really grabbed the attention though were the lights of a car. Eliot had used such a long exposure that the red tail lights were blurred and formed a long, thin streak through the picture. The effect was as though the car had careered down the slope at incredible speed. In fact she remembered it travelling at a particularly cautious rate. She'd been aware of that because she'd waited impatiently for it to be out of view.

"That's fantastic, it would never have occurred to me to include the car or make a feature of the road."

"Normally you'd be right not to, but occasionally it's good to break a few rules, do something unexpected."

"It really works. And you knew it would look like this when you took it?"

"I had this in mind, yes. Remember you asked about lead in lines?"

"Yes."

"This isn't quite that, but it gives you the idea. See how you're kind of drawn to the start of the road, well the start from our point of view?"

"Yes and then led down into the valley as though following the car. Is that what you mean?"

He made a few clicks on the computer. "This is the original image. I cropped it a bit tighter and turned it slightly. Do you see why?"

"Yes, yes I do. I see it now, but I'm not sure I'd have seen to take the shot in the first place. Can you teach me that?"

"I'm not sure I can, you either see things, or you don't."

"And do I?"

"I think maybe you do." He clicked again. "This is yours; tell me why you took it."

"That rock formation there, it seemed to match the clouds above, almost as though they were a reflection."

"Good, so how will you make the most of that?"

"Crop it a bit tighter?" she suggested.

"Go on."

That wasn't easy. She recognised the crop tool on his editing program even though it wasn't the same version she used. She wasn't used to his computer, or to being watched so closely while she worked. An even bigger problem was having to reach across Eliot to use the touch-pad. She could feel the warmth of his chest on her arm and feel his breath on her neck.

"Nice," he murmured.

She had to remind herself he was talking about the photograph.

"Is that OK?" she asked when she'd finished. Maybe she shouldn't be seeking his approval as she could see for herself it was an improvement. She stayed where she was, unwilling to move back to the position where she'd be close to him, but not close enough to touch.

"It's better, but there's more you could do."

The picture, he was still talking about the picture. "I don't see what."

"Think about reflections."

She was. Jess wondered if she turned round she would see her face reflected in his eyes and if she could, would she look as needy as she felt.

"If this really were a reflection, how would it look?"

"In a lake or something you mean?"

"It's what you meant, Jess. What you saw when you took it."

"I suppose I was thinking of water. But in that case the horizon would be… oh!"

She rotated the image so a strata of rock was horizontal across the image, suggesting a shoreline and the dark depths of water below. "A reflection!" She turned and kissed his cheek. "Thank you. Thank you for letting me do that."

"You saw it and made it happen. Know what you've seen and you can learn how to extract that image from the picture."

Jess didn't trust herself to stay so close to Eliot without touching him or trying to kiss him again. She had no idea if he'd enjoy that and didn't want to risk making things awkward with unwelcome advances.

"I need the bathroom…" he said and slid off the seat.

Huh, so the restlessness she thought she'd detected was nothing to do with him enjoying being so close to her eager body. "OK. Gosh, look at the time. We'd better go to bed."

After he'd briefly used the facilities, Jess washed herself with the absolute minimum of water, as Eliot had instructed her, and changed into her pyjamas. That gave her time to be grateful she'd not given in to temptation and kissed him again.

When she came out of the tiny bathroom Eliot had put

away the glasses and computers but not assembled her bed.

"How does this work?" Jess asked, pointing to the bench.

"Not a clue. I've never had to use it before."

Jess tried not to wonder if that was because he'd always travelled alone, or because his companion shared his bed. As he washed and brushed his teeth, she lifted the cushions, but couldn't see any levers or catches which looked as though they'd transform the bench into a bed. She was still fiddling about when Eliot emerged from the bathroom. He was wearing nothing but a tiny, snug fitting pair of shorts.

"Oh!" she gasped.

"What are you doing?" he asked.

"Trying to work out how the bed works."

"Ah, OK." He came and looked. "Not exactly obvious, is it?"

"Do you think the table has to come out first?"

"Maybe. If we open up the door it's going to get freezing in here. You'd better share with me."

"What?"

"There's no need to look so horrified. You've got your sleeping bag, haven't you?"

"Yes, but…"

"It's just sharing the space, not actually sleeping with me."

"OK." She knew she sounded uncertain.

"For goodness' sake, Jessica! Having you along wasn't my idea, so don't start acting as though you've been lured here so I can pounce on you. Trust me, that is not going to happen." He climbed up onto the bed and pulled the duvet over himself.

"I didn't mean…" Maybe better not to admit that her reluctance was simply because she didn't want to be quite so close to temptation.

Jess awkwardly scrambled into her sleeping bag and was soon lying beside him. Close enough to smell his toothpaste.

It was cosy in the van and they'd had a lovely evening. She had to fight the urge to snuggle up to Eliot. Even so she was near enough to hear his breathing, or even reach out and touch him. She definitely wasn't going to do that. As though to remind herself not to, she slid her arms down inside her sleeping bag.

As she lay there pretending to be asleep she had the impression he was doing the same.

"Rise and shine, Jessica. We're burning daylight here."

"Already?" It didn't feel like time to get up. Actually it seemed like the middle of the night, especially as inside the van it was completely dark.

"I did say there would be early starts." He switched on a light and disappeared into the bathroom.

Just like last night she could hear his every movement, even down to the zipper as he opened his washbag. He must have heard her using the facilities too. She hadn't realised quite how intimate, not always in a good way, it would be for the two of them to share such a small space.

He had warned her and she said she'd cope. This was all part of the job and she'd do it with a smile.

"There you go, all yours," Eliot said as he emerged damp from the shower, wearing only a towel.

"Great! What are we doing today? Going to the beach?"

"We're doing what we came here for – working."

"I didn't mean…"

"Don't forget about the water. Get wet, switch the shower off to wash, then a quick rinse."

Positioning the shower curtain was fiddly and it stuck to her, all cold and clammy. The water had hardly got warm before she thought she'd better switch it off. Once she'd lathered her hair and body she turned the lever round to the hottest setting before letting the water flow again. Immediately she was almost scalded. The shampoo which did get rinsed out only seemed to make it as far as her eyes before she gave up and applied the conditioner. She didn't dare use much as if she did and couldn't rinse it all out it would be sticky and uncomfortable all day.

She adjusted the temperature setting again and had three seconds of pleasantly warm water before she got an icy blast which made her shriek. "I'm OK," she yelled, just in case Eliot thought she'd got hurt and burst in to her rescue.

"I rather thought you were," he replied. "There can't be much wrong with anyone who can make as much noise as that."

She didn't reply. She absolutely refused to have an argument with someone through a door while she was naked.

Jess brushed her teeth standing in an inch of tepid water, then got dried as well as she could. It was almost impossible as everything she touched was wet.

The serum to smooth her hair was still in a bag in the back of the van, but wouldn't have helped much if applied when it was so wet. She moisturised, with night cream again as she'd accidentally brought two pots of that and no day cream. The mirror was steamed up so she couldn't see to do her make-up. Probably just as well as she suspected the alternating hot and cold water had given her a blotchy red face. She dabbed a little concealer under her eyes, as the early start was bound to have given her bags or dark circles, or both, and blended it in well. She didn't risk putting anything but gloss on her lips. Then she combed her sopping hair as well as she could and got dressed. The sleeve of her sweater had draped onto the bathroom floor, so that was wet, as were her trousers by the time she'd got them on. She wasn't in the best of moods.

Jess reminded herself this was the first day on the job she'd talked herself into and wanted to keep until the end of this trip at least. She tried to conjure up a positive mood and put on a smile, but he'd better not make any sarcastic comments about her pathetic attempts to look presentable.

Eliot had made them both a mug of coffee. "If I'd known you'd take this long I'd have woken you half an hour earlier."

"I can't have been more than fifteen minutes," she protested.

"Drink up; I don't want to waste another fifteen."

She gulped down the drink and rinsed the mug. An electronic beeping started up the moment she switched on the tap.

"What's that?" she asked.

"An alarm to say the water's low."

"Already?"

"I did say there wasn't much."

"You did, but…" But what? He had said that and now seemed ready for a row. She couldn't see that she'd done anything wrong. In fact she'd been remarkably calm about the difficulties she'd faced that morning. Maybe there was a problem she didn't know about or maybe he was always this grumpy in the mornings. Either way, she wasn't intending to spoil the day with petty arguments. "I'll try to get better at using less. Will we be able to refill today?"

"I suppose so."

"Great. OK, I'm ready." Jess grabbed her jacket and opened the side door. It was still almost completely dark outside.

Eliot followed her out and round to the rear of the van. He handed her a carrier bag, her backpack and a tripod, then put on his own backpack.

"Come on, then." He marched off across the field, climbed a stile and set off up a steep, rocky path without looking back. Jess did up her own pack, and followed carrying his tripod. She was out of breath by the time she caught up. She deliberately hung back a little so he couldn't hear her puffing.

She discovered the purpose of the carrier bag when he stooped to pick up a soggy cigarette pack, which he handed to her. "Collect what you can get to without leaving the path."

Jess remembered sighing over the litter in Capri, but walking right by it. Someone else's rubbish had, until then, seemed like someone else's problem. Clearly it wasn't just herself she was going to have to learn to accept responsibility for, if she really wanted to do this kind of work.

Eliot stopped after about forty minutes of brisk climbing. By then Jess's heart was racing, her thighs felt tight and hot and her back was sweating under the heavy gear. In contrast, her head was freezing thanks to her wet hair and her hands were cold and aching where they were holding the metal tripod. Eliot wasn't even breathing fast and seemed completely comfortable. She was tempted to throw his tripod down at his feet but that would be childish. She'd promised to help carry things, so that's what she'd do without complaining.

Eliot unpacked his camera and attached a lens.

"What are we photographing here?" Jess asked.

"I'm teaching you about the light. You did want to learn?" He challenged her to disagree.

"Yes." Her voice was meek.

There was no doubt now that Eliot was angry with her. She had no idea why and no idea what to do about the situation. She was used to people going out of their way to be nice to her, even if sometimes it was just because they wanted something from her or because they were being paid to do as she wanted. The only person who hadn't behaved like that was Tanya and, as she'd admitted, that was just because she was jealous.

Eliot seemed to be making it pretty clear he didn't want anything from Jess. She didn't understand why he should be nasty to her though. Wasn't he getting what he wanted from Daddy by bringing her on this trip? He couldn't be jealous of her either, she didn't think. He was successful and talented. He could make a lot of money if he accepted the requests from celebrities to have him promote them. Money didn't seem to be what motivated him. Jess had to admit she didn't know anyone like him and didn't understand him at all.

That was something she would have to put right – and soon.

Chapter 9

The sky had grown lighter as they'd climbed up the steep path. Jess saw they'd parked in a valley with dark, jagged peaks rising up all around them. It was still too dark to see much detail or differentiate colours, but she could tell the landscape was impressive. Just to her left there was a brighter, warmer part of the sky. The sun must be just about to rise into view.

As the sun inched over the shards of rock, Jess and Eliot took photographs. Eliot was right, the light changed continuously. It was almost as though the rocks were enchanted into sleep and the kiss of the sunlight brought them to life. Gradually colours appeared and she saw plants and patterns. Soon the chill of the night evaporated and a landscape which had seemed barren and almost sinister was rich, vibrant and alive.

Entranced, Jess almost forgot to take photographs. She wanted to look around her, take everything in and not be restricted to glimpses through her viewfinder. She wanted the landscape to surround her, not for it to be controlled and cropped and framed into one pretty view.

"It's wonderful," she said.

It wasn't until she saw Eliot nod she realised she'd spoken aloud.

"That's about it, I think, for golden hour." He didn't sound exactly friendly, but his tone wasn't as angry as before. Maybe he simply wasn't a morning person?

They packed up their gear without speaking and set off back down the hill. Jess carried the unused tripod. Walking downhill wasn't so physically demanding and she felt thoroughly cold and miserable by the time they reached the van. She considered changing her clothes as her trousers were still damp in places, but when she used the toilet she discovered the bathroom floor was still swimming in water. She pointed this out to Eliot.

"Did you undo the drain?" he asked.

"That would be difficult as I didn't know there was one," she snapped.

His look made her feel like an idiot. Of course it was obvious there would be a means of letting the water drain away. What she'd meant was that she hadn't known there was something she was supposed to do to make that happen. She guessed he knew that and she'd only seem all the more stupid if she tried to explain.

Eliot turned over a corner of the rubber matting and pulled a small plastic handle. Immediately the water began to drain away. She didn't ask why he'd closed it before she used the shower. There was still no point her going in to change her trousers as the floor was still wet. She just swapped jumpers.

Jess cooked breakfast while Eliot downloaded their shots.

"You're framing things too tightly," was the only comment he made.

"Can you show me?" she asked.

"Don't want to take my word for it?"

"I'm sure you're right, but if I see it for myself it will be easier for me to understand what I should have done."

"Fair enough." He showed her a picture. "It's framed

fine for a finished shot, but you haven't allowed any room for error. If you'd needed to straighten it you'd have nothing to play with."

"Right. Good job I got it level and it doesn't need to be straightened then."

"Can I smell burning?"

The fried eggs weren't burned, but they were a bit overcooked. Served him right and made little difference to her. He clearly wouldn't have offered a word of praise or thanks even if they, like the rest of the meal, were perfect.

She sat down to eat.

"I'd like some orange juice," Eliot said.

Because of where they were sitting it was much easier for her to fetch it than him and she supposed getting everything ready for breakfast was part of what she'd agreed to do, but she didn't like the way he just mentioned it then carried on eating as though he knew she'd jump up and get it.

She poured them both a glass, so he didn't have the satisfaction of thinking she'd got it solely for his benefit.

Jess had just sat down to eat again when he remarked that she hadn't put out the salt. Surely he didn't really need it on salty bacon, especially as everything had been cooked in the same pan and was therefore coated in the brine that came from the meat? She fought down the urge to say something and fetched the salt.

He took it from her without a word and shook it just twice over his egg.

"You're welcome," Jess said and gave him a sunny smile when he looked up.

"Oh, yes. Thanks."

After washing up from breakfast and cleaning the tiny

kitchen area, Jess carefully dried and moisturised her hands.

"Don't forget to wipe down the bathroom," Eliot said. "If it's not kept completely dry it'll start to smell and develop mildew."

Jess thoroughly dried the small space then asked brightly, "Right, what's next?" He was in a bad mood, but he needn't think he could drag her into an argument.

"Photography."

"Right. Will you be using the tripod this time?"

"Depends on the weather. Looks like it might rain, so you'd better bring the brolly as well."

After a trudge along the valley, Eliot was soon proved right about the weather. The tripod remained unused, but not the umbrella. That was needed to protect the camera equipment, whilst Jess's almost dry hair received a refreshing rainwater rinse. It wasn't much consolation that it was just a shower.

Jess assumed bad visibility was the reason they didn't stay long enough to take more than a couple of pictures, but the speed with which he returned and his impatience at waiting for her to reach the van and stow away her own and his equipment suggested otherwise. He was already in the driving seat with the engine running when she got back in the van.

"In a hurry, are we?"

"Take your coat off, you'll get the seat wet," he said.

She did and then asked as cheerfully as she could manage where they were going.

"To meet someone who co-ordinated a beach clean, and organise a photoshoot."

He pulled away before she'd done up her seat belt.

Shooting someone was beginning to sound quite appealing as he drove across the field before making a sharp turn into the lane that led to the road. When he cornered there was a loud clunk behind them and then a crashing sound. Jess looked back to see the fridge door had come open and the contents were rolling over the floor.

Eliot swore under his breath and stopped the van. Without a word, Jess undid her seat belt, climbed through into the living area and began putting things away. She could feel the silent anger coming from Eliot. It would have been easier for her if he'd shouted at her for not securing the door correctly because that way she could have shouted back that it was a simple mistake that anyone, even one as perfect as he no doubt was, could have made.

She was shivering with both cold and anger as she returned to her seat.

He drove them a short distance to the sea and then along a coast road above a glorious stretch of golden sand. They pulled into an empty car park.

As soon as Eliot stopped the vehicle, he jumped out and strode away. Jess grabbed the keys, climbed out and locked the van before following him down a narrow path and on to the beach.

He greeted an elderly man in a friendly manner. "Llewellyn, a pleasure." They shook hands.

"Great to meet you at last, Eliot, although I feel as though we know each other already."

"There have been quite a few emails going back and forward, I admit," Eliot agreed.

"There's that, but I've been looking you up. When I mentioned you were going to photograph us and our efforts, to the rest of the group, it seemed like I was the only one who'd never heard of you. Felt silly about that and sorry, by the way."

Eliot, looking embarrassed, waved away the apology. "I'm just a photographer, there's no reason you should have heard of me."

"You're proper famous though! I've been reading up about the work you did out in Thailand. That was just amazing. Don't remember reading any mention of a pretty girlfriend though." Llewellyn gestured toward Jess.

"She is NOT my girlfriend!"

"Oh sorry, put my foot in it again," Llewellyn said.

"Hi, I'm Jessica Borlase," Jess said offering her hand.

"Nice to meet you, my dear, and sorry about my misunderstanding. No offence meant."

"None taken," Jess said. She was annoyed with Eliot for not introducing her and then sounding so alarmed Llewellyn might think the pair of them were an item, but she felt she'd scored a point by making it clear it was she and not Eliot who should be offended by that suggestion. "I'm just the lowly assistant, here to fetch and carry things whilst he trains me to take a decent photograph."

"I think he's lucky to have you."

"Thank you, it's nice to be appreciated." Jess was getting to like Llewellyn. Shame he was twice Daddy's age, or she could have given Eliot a reason for the thunderous look which clouded his face.

"So, is Friday still all right for the shoot?" Eliot asked.

"Certainly is. I've checked the weather forecast and it promises to be good weather. I hope that stays until the Bank Holiday as we're having a barbecue then. If you're still in the area, we'd be honoured if you could join us.

Both of you, of course."

"I'm not sure…" Eliot started to say.

"We're not going back until next week," Jess interrupted, just because she could tell he was being evasive. He obviously didn't want to give an outright no, just as he wasn't prepared to say what she'd done to annoy him.

"We will be in Wales then, but not necessarily in Pembrokeshire. Thanks for the offer though, it does sound like fun. OK if we let you know later?"

"No problem. It's supposed to be a pretty informal affair so one or two more or less shouldn't make much difference."

"Great, thanks. Well, we'd better look at this beach then and see how we're going to tackle it."

They all walked back and forth along the water's edge and Llewellyn indicated the work which had been done and described how it had looked before. Eliot's grumpiness had vanished and he was charming to Llewellyn as the two men strolled ahead of Jess. Eliot gave just the right amount of praise for the restoration work; enough for Llewellyn to feel good, but not so much it seemed like empty flattery.

She was kind of glad neither of them asked her opinion as she couldn't see how to photograph the project other than with straightforward shots of the work which had been done. They couldn't even contrast it with places where the land was being eroded into the sea as everywhere which had needed attention had received it. She guessed from what she'd heard that the job had been hard work, but you couldn't really tell from the neat edging of wooden railway sleepers. To her it didn't look much more ambitious than a large scale garden makeover.

They said goodbye to Llewellyn eventually and Eliot drove through the town. They stopped to buy sandwiches which they took back to the field they'd camped in overnight. Jess made tea to drink with them. Eliot took big angry bites and gulped his tea. It seemed as though he were filling his mouth in order to avoid speaking to her, but perhaps she was being fanciful.

"In a hurry?" she asked.

"Sort of. I want to get back up the hill again reasonably soon. We need more water and that'll take a while, then we've got to go back up again for golden hour this evening."

"We're going back up the mountain we climbed first thing this morning?"

"It's a hill, and yes we are."

"Twice more today?"

"That's right." He sounded as though he were explaining something to a particularly dull child.

"But you said the light at midday isn't very good."

"That's right. I said it because it's true, but you need to see it for yourself."

She wouldn't give him the satisfaction of admitting he didn't need to prove it to her. She didn't doubt he was right, but didn't feel like saying so at that moment and in any case, she'd understand better if she did see it for herself.

After lunch they climbed back up the path they'd walked that morning. It seemed even harder the second time, especially as she knew the photos wouldn't be so good. Her leg muscles felt hard and uncomfortable long before she reached the top. Thank goodness she hadn't bought new boots which would surely have been rubbing her feet by now. Even with her worn in ones and proper walking socks, her heels were feeling a little warm.

Jess didn't have to wait to see the photographs on her laptop, she could tell as she took them that they wouldn't have the drama of the earlier ones. If she'd come at midday first, she'd have been happily snapping away and thought the images good, but Eliot was right. Earlier in the day the light had been different and much better. She moved away from him, sat on the cold earth and tried not to look as fed up as she felt, and so give Eliot an excuse to claim he'd been right to say she wouldn't enjoy the trip.

"Jess, come here," he hissed.

Reluctantly she hauled herself up and took the tripod over to him. "Here you…"

"Shh." He gestured for her to come closer. "There, just behind that darker patch of heather." He put one arm around her shoulder and pointed in front of them.

Jess stared at the spot. It was just heather and maybe some dead leaves until she saw a movement. A fawn! All she could see was the head and a few spots on its back. No, there was another. "Twins?" she whispered.

"It's not uncommon with roe deer."

Maybe not, but she'd never seen even a single before, or an adult at anything like such a close range. She'd never have seen these if he hadn't pointed them out to her.

"Are you going to photograph them?" she asked. Her own camera was still in the spot where she'd sat to sulk.

"No, they're too well camouflaged to make a good shot. Come on, we'd better leave them to it."

As they moved away, Jess asked if they'd scared off the mother.

"Probably not. I thought I saw a deer as we climbed up,

but wasn't sure." He explained the harts kept the fawns hidden in grass, bracken or heather for about three months, returning to suckle them several times a day. "They're safer kept hidden until they're strong enough to keep up with the herd."

As soon as they'd climbed back down again, Eliot stowed their camera gear and jumped into the driver's seat. He hadn't told Jess they were off, so she'd been in the back and had to hurriedly scramble into the front, banging her knee painfully as she did so.

Eliot stopped the van outside a churchyard in a lane. "There are always taps in churchyards, so people can fill the flower vases."

Ah yes, they were refilling with water, because she'd rashly spent two whole minutes in the shower. Jess felt a little uncomfortable about taking water intended for such a purpose. They had to carry containers quite a way and hold them up to the tap while they were filling, then carry them back to the van and pour the water into the tank via a large plastic funnel. That part was even more uncomfortable, though in a different way. They had to work together to use the funnel as it needed two hands to hold the water containers up high and empty them, and the funnel had to be held into position. It was impossible to do this without bodily contact.

Jess could only just lift up the container she'd been given and as she held it to let the water gurgle out, her arms shook with the effort. "How do you manage on your own?" she asked.

"Awkwardly." He took the half empty container from her and demonstrated. "But then I need less than half the water when I'm on my own."

Naturally he couldn't answer a simple question without

reminding her how inconvenient it was to have her there!

"Would you rather hold the funnel?" Eliot offered.

"It's fine. I'll be using the water, so I should pour it in." She was very glad though that when her container was empty he handed the funnel to her.

Eliot made light work of emptying his own container, even though it was twice the size of hers. If he did that regularly, after a day lugging all his equipment about, it explained him being so fit and strong.

They returned to the tap and refilled the containers twice more. Jess's hands got cold as water splashed over them and soon her arms were aching as much as her legs. As she brought the container back towards the van for the last time, it slipped from her hand. The top popped off and water gushed upwards, soaking her legs and feet. She wanted to cry out in frustration. Even the laws of physics were against her. She looked up to see Eliot grinning.

"You so much as think about laughing and what's left goes over you!"

"Wouldn't dream of laughing. It's not funny at all."

She trudged back the rest of the way and hefted up the container to pour what was left into the funnel Eliot was holding steady. As the last trickle of water came out she dropped her arms in relief. The edge of the container banged against the still full funnel, spraying icy water in an arc over Eliot.

As the cold water hit him, Eliot looked as shocked as though she'd punched him.

Chapter 10

She probably should have felt guilty, but all Jess could think of was that he deserved it and how good he looked with his wet T-shirt clinging to his chest. Not feeling guilty didn't mean she wouldn't have been willing to pull his wet clothing off and rub him dry with a big fluffy towel. If she tried doing that he'd probably look a lot more shocked than he did already.

Eliot hadn't moved. He just stood, water dripping down him, staring at the funnel, which he'd instinctively caught, as though wondering how it had ended up upside down in his hand, its contents soaking his body. Perhaps he'd think she'd done it deliberately. She'd better put him right.

"That was an accident, Eliot. I might be as annoying as you obviously consider me, but I can't take credit for drenching you. I'm too tired to have thought of it."

Eliot bit his lip, presumably to stop him making a rude remark.

Jess turned to go back for more water as she'd spilled half of the last lot she'd carried.

"Wait, Jessica," he said.

"Have we got enough?" she asked.

"I think we've both had enough," he said. "You go and get some dry clothes on, I'll put this lot away."

Jess quickly changed into dry jeans and socks. She changed her jumper too as the sleeves were sopping wet.

Luckily the bathroom floor was perfectly dry by then. She rubbed in hand cream, brushed her windblown hair and applied lipsalve. Jess felt much better once she was dry, tidy and starting to get warm.

Eliot was already in the van when she emerged from the tiny bathroom, and halfway through getting changed. He was wearing nothing but his black underpants, and a smile as he saw her staring at him.

"Sorry," she mumbled although she wasn't quite sure what this apology was for.

"No problem."

She had to stay there and watch him towel himself dry, just as she'd imagined doing to him, and then put on his clothes. There was nowhere else for her to go. If she'd pushed past him and sat on the bench seat she'd have got an even closer view. Somehow it wasn't until he'd almost finished that it occurred to her to stare out of the window.

"Right then, up the hill again for more shots in the evening sun," he said when he was dressed. He drove them back to where they'd camped overnight.

Jess tried to think about something other than the pain in her legs as she climbed. It was a good plan in theory, but maybe not wise as the only thing which filled her mind was the sight of Eliot getting dressed. The deep tan on his face and arms seemed to cover the whole of his body. If he'd been wearing anything at all in the sun it must have been an extremely brief pair of trunks as the underwear she'd seen earlier hadn't left much to the imagination. Annoyingly that didn't stop her imagination from working. It wondered how soft the black material might feel and what Eliot's reaction might have been if she'd run her hand down his chest, over the firm muscles of his flat abdomen and then down lower, to find out.

She really should have been more careful with the water container. Jess was paying the price of her carelessness just as much as he had from the soaking she'd given him. She almost giggled as she recalled his shocked gasp as the icy water slapped into his face and down the length of his body.

"Eliot, I really am sorry about splashing you. I admit I was tempted to give you a good soaking, but I really didn't do that on purpose."

He stopped and turned to face her. "OK, I believe you."

They managed a brief smile at each other before he said they'd better hurry to catch the best of the light.

The light probably was good when they stopped to take pictures, but Jess didn't have the strength to appreciate it. Her legs didn't want to hold her body steady and her arms were having the same difficulty with the camera. She pointed and clicked almost at random, more to stop Eliot wondering why she wasn't shooting than through any hope of getting a worthwhile result. She walked back down again feeling like a zombie. When Eliot stopped and looked back at her she almost crashed into him.

"Keep going," she said. "If I stop, I'm not sure my legs will start again."

"Am I pushing you too hard?"

"I can cope," she snapped and instantly regretted it. He'd sounded genuinely concerned.

Jess was exhausted by the time they got back to the van, yet still cleaned her camera equipment and packed it ready for the morning. One thing Eliot couldn't criticise was the way she looked after her kit. Just as he did, Jess always polished every lens before putting it away and used a lens cloth regularly to ensure there was never a speck of dust, spot of moisture or stray hair to spoil a shot. Once that was done, she would happily have gone straight to sleep. That wasn't possible as Eliot had opened up his laptop on the table which was needed to make the single bed.

"More work?" she asked.

"It's important to keep on top of processing. Shots are no good still in the camera and you need to back everything up. Plus if there's a problem of any kind you can get it fixed before the next job."

Served her right for asking. She'd been hoping he was playing solitaire on a purely working trip and she could score a point, not looking for another lecture.

If she couldn't sleep, she might as well eat. Her legs felt as though they were going into spasm as she bent to remove food from the fridge and cupboards. She spotted chicken breasts, a jar of spicy tomato sauce and there were wholemeal pasta shells. Too bad if he didn't want pasta again, cooking it would be easy. Standing wasn't, she had to hold onto the cooker hob to haul herself upright.

"You OK?" he asked.

"Why wouldn't I be?" Oh dear, that too had sounded defensive. Perhaps if she'd found a way to explain how tired she was without sounding like she was complaining, he'd ease up a little?

"If you're not used to climbing, your muscles must be stiff. Shall I show you some stretching exercises?"

It would probably have been a good idea if she'd had the strength for that. "Thanks, but later." She attempted a brave smile. Moaning wouldn't do her any good. He'd made it clear the trip was a working one and she'd said she'd do her share. She wasn't about to admit he'd been right about how hard it would be for her.

Jess put water to boil for the pasta and sliced the

chicken and an onion. Once they were sizzling in a dash of olive oil she tried to open the jar of sauce. It wouldn't budge. Eliot was trying not to smirk, so she realised she was doing something wrong. She looked down at the tin in her hand. A tin? Why had she thought it was a jar? She found the can opener, removed the lid and dumped the contents into the frying pan. Instead of the expected sauce, baked beans spilled out. Not just beans, there were lumps of something else.

Jess studied the tin. 'Breakfast in a Can' it said. Beans, mini sausages and bacon pieces. What a revolting idea. What a stupid man Eliot was to have brought it and put it where she could mix it up with pasta sauce. Stupid, stupid man. Well, he was going to have to eat it, she simply didn't have the energy left to start again. She'd have to eat it too. Once the food was cooking her stomach had begun to gurgle like crazy and she guessed her weakness was partly due to lack of food.

Eliot found a photo of hers which wasn't straight and mentioned it. She'd been so tired it was a mystery to her how any of them could be straight. She didn't say so.

Jess forced her legs to hold her steady long enough to strip a handful of basil from her plant. Maybe a garnish would dissuade him from commenting on the unusual combination of ingredients. As she tore the fragrant basil and scattered it over the chicken and bean mixture, Eliot shut down the laptop. She found the colander to drain the pasta only to have it disappear from her hand.

"Here, let me," Eliot said. He drained the pasta and tipped half onto each of the plates which had magically placed themselves on the now clear table. She was so tired she allowed him to push her onto the seat and took a glass of wine from him before she fully understood that she wasn't hallucinating, he was helping her. She was so grateful she nearly cried.

"This smells delicious," he said as he forked up a large mouthful.

He was right, it did smell good thanks to the basil. It didn't look terrible, just odd. Jess ate a small piece. It didn't taste that bad. Better than if she'd selected pineapple chunks instead of beans which she seemed to remember was what lay the other side of the pasta sauce.

They ate their supper without speaking. Jess was about to ask him to stop sulking when she saw he was struggling to keep his eyes open and trying hard not to yawn. Of course he was tired too. He'd walked the same distance, his backpack was far heavier than hers and he'd carried much more water as well as doing the driving.

When they'd eaten they sat and finished the wine as though neither of them had the strength to move. She'd have liked to say something to make friends, but didn't have the energy to try.

"I'm leaving the washing up until the morning," she announced and hauled herself into the bathroom. She stripped as the sink slowly filled with water and then dipped in her sponge and squeezed it hard so warm water could run down her aching shoulders and back. The water was ice cold. Jess squealed.

"Sorry, I forgot to put the water heater on," Eliot called.

"Like hell you did!" This was his way of getting back at her for drenching him earlier. How childish could a man be?

"Are you annoyed with me?" Eliot asked.

"Your photographer's eye for detail never lets you down, does it?"

When she came out of the bathroom the single bed still

hadn't been set up. She again tried to find a mechanism which would allow her to do that. "Does this van actually have another berth?"

"I told you it did."

"Then how do you assemble it?"

"I don't know. I didn't imagine I'd need to."

"Oh really? Well, I'm not that kind of girl."

"Don't be so damn stupid. Or so vain. I know you're not a tart and I'm not the slightest bit interested in you anyway. I just wasn't expecting to have you with me."

"Oh." That was pretty much what he'd said the night before and to make matters worse, he had a point. Jess had assumed he wanted her sleeping next to him and hadn't put up the single bed for that reason. She didn't think she was vain, but she was used to men being attracted to her. She told him so.

"Attracted to you, or to what your father can do for them?"

"Get them trained and set up in a career, you mean?"

She could tell she'd hurt him as badly as he'd hurt her, but it wasn't any consolation. They glared at each other for a few moments.

"I know you're as annoyed with me as I am with you, Jessica, but if you're going to stay then we have to put that behind us and be professional, no matter what our feelings. There's no room in the van, or time on the trip, for anything else."

He must be wondering how many times he had to tell her this was a working trip and nothing else. She climbed up onto the bed and wriggled into her sleeping bag.

Jess woke in a panic the next morning; she was being held

tight and couldn't move and didn't know where she was. Something metal was digging into her face. She thrashed about madly trying to break free.

"Hey, shush… it's just a bad dream," a soothing voice told her.

She lay still, catching her breath.

"It's OK now, Jess. Just a dream."

It was Eliot's voice and he was stroking her hair. She was in the van with him in Wales. Her sleeping bag was wrapped tightly round her and the zip was across her face. He must have been holding her when she woke up. Presumably he'd been sleeping too and had a shock to wake and find her hysterical in his arms.

"OK?" he asked.

"Yes, fine." She wanted to leap out of bed and away from the embarrassment of having him comfort her, but her breathing was still shallow and rapid and the sleeping bag was still wrapped around her. Her exit wouldn't be quick or dignified.

"I'm hot," she wriggled as far away from him as she could without rolling onto the floor, which left a gap of about an inch and a half between them. She fiddled about undoing the zip.

Eliot pushed back the blind covering the skylight over the bed. "Looks like it's going to be sunny today."

He was right. Already it was brighter than it had been as they ate their peculiar supper the previous night.

"What time is it?"

"Nearly seven."

Really? It didn't feel as though she'd got any rest at all. Jess was about to apologise for oversleeping when it occurred to her he was still in bed and could easily have woken her if he'd wanted to. She wasn't going to let him give her the blame for missing his precious golden hour.

She crawled out of the sleeping bag and into the bathroom, where she stripped off her sweaty pyjamas. She'd carried the water, she was entitled to use it. She let it run into the sink to drown out the sound as she used the toilet, then quickly switched the lever over to shower mode and dived under the tepid water. Jess just rinsed her hair. Her aching arms didn't possess the strength to shampoo and condition it.

Cold, tired and feeling grubby, Jess dried herself and then realised she'd forgotten to bring any clothes in with her. Wrapped in towels she stepped out of the bathroom. Eliot was still in bed, so she'd either have to climb back up next to him and lean across to look into the overhead lockers or ask him to pass her clothes down to her. She chose the second option.

"Sure, what do you want?"

"A T-shirt, jeans and jumper from that one."

He took out one of each and held them up for her approval.

She nodded then pointed to the next locker, which was the one he'd reserved for her use. "And underwear." She had to watch him sort through the contents to find a matching bra and knickers.

Jess could see he was keeping his face rigid and trying to show no reaction. She returned to the bathroom to get dressed. Now she'd spend all day with him knowing she was wearing palest blue French knickers and matching lacy bra. Hopefully that would make him feel as uncomfortable as it did her.

Chapter 11

"We've already missed the morning light, so there's no rush to get going. Let's have a proper breakfast, shall we?"

"Unlike yesterday's you mean? Or was that a dig about last night's dinner? I said I'd cook and I'm doing my best even though the facilities are cramped and I didn't choose the ingredients. I don't expect thanks, but there's no need to…"

"Jess, I wasn't complaining," he interrupted.

"No?" It had sounded that way to her.

"It's just that yesterday we had to go straight out before you'd even had a chance to finish your coffee."

"Oh, well…"

"And I'm sorry I was so hard on you yesterday."

"Why were you?"

"It seemed as though you hadn't got the message about being here to work…"

"I told you I was. I don't see why that has to mean we can't at least try to enjoy the scenery and stuff too."

He nodded. "And I hadn't slept well, and umm I'm not used to sharing my space."

He was going to have to get used to it as she wasn't going to let his grumpiness beat her. "Me neither. Good thing we'll be working outside most of the time."

Eliot made an expression which might have meant agreement or even an apology. She decided to take it as both. Everything would be so much easier for them both if they were on friendlier terms.

He picked up a cushion and settled himself in the driver's seat, which was still turned around to face the table. He must have noticed her flat was decorated in the same turquoise shade as the cushions, towels and interior trim of his van, but so far neither of them had mentioned the fact. Jess decided to remind him, and point out that and her attention to detail proved they had more in common than he thought.

"Was it difficult to find cushions to exactly match the van?" she asked.

"Lizzie gave them to me. She's got a good eye for colour."

"Lizzie did?" That meant they were probably Jess's cast offs. Lizzie bought some for her when she'd moved into her own apartment. Jess, resenting what she saw as interference and determination to push her out of the main part of the house, refused the gift. She'd ended up buying some which looked just as good, but were decorated with sequins, so couldn't really be used without the risk of snagging her clothes or spoiling them.

"I wouldn't have bothered getting any myself, as they take up space, but I have to admit they're comfortable."

"Er, yes." Jess didn't say anything else until she announced, "Breakfast is ready."

She served up perfect scrambled eggs and smoked salmon on hot buttered toast and dusted with paprika she'd brought with her. Usually she'd have added chives to the mix, but as none were available she'd substituted slivers of the green part of spring onions. The dainty rings looked so pretty she'd do the same in future. Jess placed the plates on the table next to the cafetière of coffee, glasses of orange juice and pots of cherry yoghurt. The table was laid with salt and pepper, paper serviettes and everything she could think of that he could possibly ask for.

"This looks great," he said as he sat down. He swallowed a mouthful of eggs. "Just how I like them."

She glanced up to see if he was being sarcastic but decided he wasn't. He did seem in a much better mood after a decent sleep. Maybe all that climbing up and down hills had been designed to help with that?

"Shall we look through yesterday's pictures?" he suggested.

"If that fits in with your timetable."

"Jess…" he pleaded.

"I don't know what you have planned for the rest of the trip," she pointed out.

"Right. Well, it makes sense to go through them now so you can put into practice anything I tell you."

That did make sense, particularly if he was only going to criticise her work and point out things to either do, or avoid doing, in the future. She washed up, in warmish water while he worked on yesterday's pictures.

As she'd predicted, he went through her shots one by one, pointing out her errors. The nearest he got to praising her was a grudging, "That's all right," for a couple of them.

He explained the difference between the light at the three different times of day, as though she couldn't possibly see that for herself.

"You'll notice I didn't take many at midday. That's because I could see they wouldn't be so good as the earlier ones," she said.

"Good," he acknowledged. "Taking pictures you don't

need wastes power, storage space and reduces the life of your equipment."

The final batch of pictures weren't very good because she'd not been concentrating on what she was doing. She had lacked the strength to hold the camera steady for long so had quickly taken shots rather than thoughtfully framing them. Her lack of attention and interest was reflected in the pictures. That was a shame because when she looked at them now she could see the light had created dramatic contrasts and interesting shadows which might have produced good images if she'd taken more trouble.

Eliot pointed out a few shots where she'd framed too tightly, leaving no room for the realigning that would have made the best of the picture.

"I was so tired I could barely press the shutter."

"Shall I run you down to the train station? You could have a nice snooze in first class."

Ah, so he'd realised she wasn't going to quit without a bit of help, had he? "A kind offer, but no thank you."

"Entirely up to you."

He then went through his own pictures, explaining what he'd done and why. Of course his were better, he was a professional with years of experience. But then that's why she was there, to learn from him, she reminded herself. This wasn't college where minimum effort was greeted with praise, nor Daddy's firm where she could do no wrong.

"Today we're going to take general stock shots of people using the beach in different ways. That has to be done during the day, as that's when the people are about. Sometimes we can't pick the 'right' time and just have to photograph things when they happen."

"Very insightful." That sounded more sarcastic than

she'd intended.

"Would it be helpful if I didn't tell you things just because to me they seem obvious? I've been doing this for years. It's not that easy to know if you'll have been taught things on your college course or found them out yourself, or if it's something new to you."

"You're right. Sorry. I suppose golden hour and lead in lines and all the rest seem obvious to you?"

"Now they do, but I had to learn. The best way is to practise. How about we go down the beach and do that?"

"Sounds great."

He drove them to a picture postcard pretty beach, full of family groups.

Eliot retrieved their backpacks from the van and handed Jess hers. "Take a wander round and shoot whatever grabs your interest. Colour, patterns, action. I expect you'll notice different things from me."

"OK." She was sure he meant exactly what he'd said. Not better or worse, just different.

She'd barely left his side when her phone rang.

"How's it going with that gorgeous man of yours?" Christina asked.

"I'm exhausted."

Christina cackled. "That's my girl!"

"Not like that! It's way harder work than I thought and I'm finding living in a campervan a bit challenging," Jess admitted.

"Oh. Shame. Is he an actual slob then, or just not quite up to your obsessive tidiness level?"

"Actually he is tidy. There's not room to be anything else. Like he said, the van isn't big enough to show our feelings for each other."

"I thought you said there was a double bed!"

Jess laughed. "One track mind you've got."

"With good reason at the moment."

"Oh?"

"A sort of souvenir from Capri. You remember Raoul?"

If Christina hadn't growled as she said the name, Jess wouldn't have recalled the slim waiter who'd been so attentive during the friends' holiday.

"He's in England?"

"Sure is. I'll explain when I see you."

Something told Jess that the explanation was going to be more erotic than gastronomic. It also occurred to her that Eliot also only had one thing on his mind most of the time; work. He wouldn't want her around if she proved a distraction, whether it was with complaints or in a way Christina would approve of.

Jess took a random selection of pictures and went to join Eliot. She waited and watched as he photographed an attractive clump of seaweed. Had he placed the bright green wispy stuff amongst the thick, brown gelatinous strands of kelp, or just spotted a piece of natural abstract art? As she couldn't tell, it wouldn't matter in the final image.

"How are you doing?" Eliot asked.

"You said you wanted people using the beach. Did you have anything specific in mind?"

"The opposite, really. With stock shots, the more variety the better. You do get a feel for what will sell, but can't always anticipate what you'll be asked for."

"So seagulls trying to nick people's lunch and kids burying Dad in the sand are OK?"

"In theory. Taking crowd scenes is fine, but you can't

use photographs of small groups or individuals without their permission, and a parent's permission as well if kids are involved. That does make things difficult sometimes. Images such as a cute kid eating an ice cream are a bit of a cliché, but can't be beaten for creating the atmosphere of a traditional family holiday."

"So, why not ask people?" Jess asked.

"It's not that simple."

"I don't see why not. You've got a printer in the van haven't you?"

"Yes, but…"

"Come on."

In a matter of minutes, Jess had created a form to allow people to give written permission for their pictures to be taken and used commercially. She printed one off for Eliot's approval. "Will that do?"

"That's great. How did you know about model release forms?"

"We had them for college. They do it automatically. It's mostly for the under eighteens but even I had to sign one."

Eliot printed a few copies and Jess approached the people he wished to photograph. Some people did say they'd rather not have the pictures taken but plenty agreed immediately and seemed pleased to have been asked.

Jess made a game out of it with the children and easily got them to pose, smile and laugh for Eliot's pictures. She knew she was being useful and contributing towards getting the results he wanted. Maybe it was that, or perhaps just the effect of being amongst a group of happy people enjoying the sunshine on a beautiful beach, but for the first time she felt easy in his company.

"Thanks for your help today, Jess," Eliot said as they

packed their gear back into the van.

"You're welcome."

"You're great with kids."

"I like them. I hope to have a few of my own one day." She blurted out that last bit without thinking. It was true, although for some reason she'd tried to tell herself that marriage and kids wasn't for her. Still, he might wonder why she felt it was appropriate to share the information with him.

"Me too. Like them I mean."

"You don't want any yourself, then?" She blushed as she finished the sentence. That wasn't the kind of personal information she'd normally exchange with a man she hardly knew, even if she had shared his bed the night before and he knew exactly what her underwear looked like.

"Not really thought about it. I've never been in the position to, you know, working away a lot."

"Never met the right woman?"

He shrugged. "Maybe there's one that's right for me, but I might not be right for her."

Jess wondered if he had a particular woman in mind. She didn't like that thought much.

As they walked back to the van, Eliot said, "There are a couple of things we need to do before we park up for the night." He didn't say it as though he expected her to be delighted at whatever he had in mind.

"More water?"

"That wouldn't hurt, but I was thinking of the toilet cassette. That needs to be emptied."

"Right. Um, where do I do that, and how?"

"A couple of jobs, I said. We need more food too. One

of us could go shopping while the other sorts out the van stuff."

"That sounds sensible." It also seemed sensible for the one who didn't know how to do that and had never driven a campervan to be dropped off at the supermarket. She'd welcome the chance to choose the food, but didn't want to sound unwilling to do the dirty job. "We could toss a coin for it?"

"Fair enough." He took one from his pocket. "Heads you go shopping, OK?"

"OK."

She didn't see how the coin landed, but as he said it was heads she didn't insist. As they pulled into the supermarket car park, Jess asked, "Anything in particular you'd like?"

He gave a wicked smile. "Breakfast foods since you seem to eat them for every meal."

"I'm not buying that stuff in a can. Once was more than enough." She gave a mock shudder at the memory.

"Whatever you can cook in the facilities we have available will be just fine with me."

Jess enjoyed selecting food which would be tasty whilst requiring the minimum of space and equipment to prepare. She guessed that awful breakfast in a can was the sort of thing he'd usually heat up for himself and knew she could do much better, even with the very limited space and equipment in the campervan.

She bought duck breast for their dinner that evening. She'd serve it with sweet, dark plum sauce and a colourful stir-fry; peppers, mange tout, carrots, red onion, chestnut mushrooms and spinach. Without the rice or noodles she couldn't face, that might be too insubstantial for Eliot, so she picked up a rich chocolate gateaux to follow. With all the work she was doing she wasn't going to have any trouble eating a slice of that herself. A big slice.

The same amount of thought went into choices for their meals over the next few days. To the food, Jess added fruit juice, three bottles of decent wine, milk and teabags. Eliot had her putting the kettle on every time they returned to the van and she had the feeling running out of tea wouldn't improve his mood. Remembering whatever she bought had to fit into the available cupboard space, Jess headed for the check out.

When she came out of the supermarket, she spotted the campervan parked in an out of the way corner, with Eliot leant against it. He was on the phone and didn't notice her until she was quite close.

"Got to go," he said and snapped it shut without listening for a reply.

Jess couldn't help feeling that he'd not wanted her listening in on his conversation, but he smiled as though pleased to see her. "Great timing, I've not been back long." He took a couple of bags from the trolley.

After Jess had removed the other one, he returned the trolley and then helped her put everything away. Helped was probably being generous as in the confined space they were mostly in each other's way.

"I think we've invented a new game; campervan twister," she said as she reached around him trying to securely stow the red wine.

"And you'll be the winner if you can find a home for the peppers and all this green stuff."

"We're eating them tonight. They'll be OK until then." Jess put the vegetables and pack of fresh coriander in the sink, next to the sparse looking basil plant. "What's my prize?"

The van was at its narrowest between the 'kitchen' sink and bathroom which was just where they were standing. Jess was pressed against him and looking up into his long lashed eyes.

Eliot bent his head as though to kiss her, then quickly straightened up again. "If you're really good, I'll show you how to use a tripod."

Chapter 12

It didn't take them long to reach their next overnight stop. Barely long enough for Jess to remember there was a phone signal, update her father on the progress of the trip and check her messages.

Zoe, Alyssa and Christina had all replied to Jess's email moaning that Eliot often either ignored her or seemed to treat her like a self-propelled piece of camera equipment. Alyssa said it probably wasn't personal, more likely he just got absorbed in his work. Christina had creative suggestions for proving Jess was a flesh and blood woman, and Zoe said it showed he was being considerate. 'Just think how awkward it would be if he made a move on you and you weren't interested.'

Alyssa and Zoe's points both made a lot of sense. All Christina's were tempting, but almost certainly unwise. Jess's phone had lost the signal before she'd replied to them all.

As Eliot downloaded their photographs, Jess prepared the stir-fry. She left the plates, cutlery and glasses in the cupboard as she sliced the meat, sprinkled it with five-spice, and returned it to the pack it had come in. That went back in the fridge so she had room to chop the vegetables, coriander and garlic. When everything was ready, she heated Eliot's large pan on the gas hob. Only when the meat was sizzling did she lay the table. She was definitely getting the hang of this!

Her hands were beginning to show she wasn't used to working though. The campervan might be small and the products Eliot had on board for cleaning it eco-friendly, but regularly wiping down the cooking area and bathroom as well as washing up after breakfasts, lunches and countless cups of tea was already taking a toll. Jess's usually immaculate nails were looking dry and the cuticles were ragged. No wonder Mrs Jennings usually wore gloves.

It had seemed practical for Jess to have the polish removed and her nails filed quite short before the trip. She'd assumed Eliot wouldn't be keen on the smell of polish or remover in the confined conditions, nor the space they'd take up. No doubt she was right about that, but she wished she had something other than regular applications of hand cream to improve how they looked. Then she remembered that for the second day in a row she had towel-dried hair and a make-up free face. Shiny fingernails wouldn't do anything to counteract that.

Eliot not only ate both the duck stir-fry and gooey chocolate cake with obvious enthusiasm, but was full of praise for her cooking and for the way she, just, managed to get everything they hadn't eaten into the fridge. He topped up their wine glasses and then, sitting next to her, ran a slideshow of the day's photos.

There were quite a few with her in them, including several where she was part of a group, playing with the children. There was a lovely one of Jess, two mothers and a group of girls', giggling together, with the males of the family just out of shot building a huge sand fortress. In another, the girls were running towards the enormous fortress which was being defended by the dads and boys. The next in the sequence showed the dads and boys scattering in all directions and two girls leaping in the air.

There were more as other women and girls jumped, the first into the air having already landed on the sand fortifications. Gradually each of them landed and all of them, even a toddler assisted by her big sister, stomped on the sand wall around the moat. The girls stood triumphant until the boys returned with water pistols. Eliot had caught a jet of water approaching Jess's head. The action was frozen a split second before the water found its target. Jess could almost hear her shriek and the laughter of the boy who'd fired.

"These are brilliant, Eliot!"

"I've got a lens designed for sporting events. It's great for anything like this."

"You must have quick reflexes to get shots like this, or physic powers or something."

"It's just a matter of watching and being ready as things happen."

"Before they happen. A great lens helps, but I've learned enough to know that's not even half the battle."

He nodded. "No, but knowing that might be."

Eliot quickly clicked through a few more pictures. Jess couldn't help noticing she was in a lot of them. That included two of just her face and another from the waist up showing the full effect of cold water on her flimsy T-shirt.

"You can delete that one!" she informed him.

"I promise it won't go on display to the public."

There were more pictures of children eating ice creams and trying to catch seagulls, of teenagers flying kites and older people on deckchairs drinking from flasks of tea and watching the action. Eliot stopped scrolling through when there were still several shots she hadn't seen.

"What's wrong with the last ones? Crooked and out of focus?"

He laughed. "Don't be silly, I'd delete any like that before you got to see them."

"Oh, I didn't think of that."

"What I mean is that in the very, very unlikely event of me taking a picture that wasn't completely perfect, I'd delete it." His grin showed he was teasing her.

She didn't suppose there were many he had to delete, but the thought cheered her a little. If she went through her shots before he saw them and deleted the ones which were obviously no good at all she'd still have quite a few and he'd be left with a lot less ammunition to criticise her. Maybe she'd try that next time.

"So, let's see them."

Eliot selected the 'deleted' file on his computer, which was far from empty. He opened some until he found a shot which really was crooked and blurry!

"I slipped on some seaweed," he said. "You can't see the rest; I don't have enough excuses ready."

Jess smiled. "That's reassuring, but actually it was the ones you've saved which I wanted to see."

He leant back to allow her to click through the shots. That didn't give her much room and she had to lean against his chest to get her face far enough from the screen to focus. It was like squinting into a mirror. They were all of her as she laughed and said goodbye to their models. She remembered how she'd felt at that moment. She'd been happy. Happier than she could remember feeling since before her mum had become ill. They were good pictures of her, she might ask him for a copy of one. She didn't know why he'd taken so many. He couldn't really use more than one picture of her in his exhibition.

"Well, you can't fault the model," she said, hoping a light-hearted comment would defuse the tension she felt in Eliot.

"You just looked so happy," he said.

Jess nodded. Had she been looking so grumpy that he'd felt a change from that expression warranted a permanent record? Quite possibly, she reflected.

"I think I've got lots of stuff I can use. That location was perfect for our purposes."

Jess smiled as she noticed he was saying 'we' now, including her in the project, perhaps not thinking of her as an equal, but certainly someone who was part of what he was doing rather than simply a hindrance.

"Yes, very scenic," she said.

"And in a particularly useful way."

"Oh? I'm not sure I follow."

"I'll show you." He brought up two photos side by side, then sat back waiting for her response.

One showed kite flying, the other was a game of Frisbee. Both were good shots. Neither showed a great deal of landscape.

"I still don't get it… mostly it's just the beach. There aren't any distinctive landmarks, they could have been taken almost anywhere in South Wales …"

"Go on."

She stared at the images. The kite showed a Welsh dragon and she'd persuaded the Frisbee players to wear 'I love Wales' tops, so it was clear where the action was happening, even if the rocky outcrop in one and the green hills in the other didn't give it away.

"I've got it! They look like different places so it seems like you've been to two different locations."

He smiled.

"And if you cropped out those clouds at the very top of that one then it would look like they were different days, too."

"Yep."

They sat companionably to finish the wine and, as they were still within wifi range, go through their emails. Jess had one from Tanya, updating her on gossip about her ex fellow students and her progress with the course. There were further thanks for the laptop. Daddy had sent her another message and for the first time she was able to send a really enthusiastic reply about how well things were going on the trip. That was rather ironic because although it was the first day she'd not actually taken many pictures she'd learned a lot and had been genuinely useful.

"Fan mail?" Eliot asked as he heard her tapping away furiously.

"Just Daddy and a friend, the rest is mostly junk."

"No boyfriend pining away for you or getting jealous that I get to pick your underwear each morning."

"No. What about you?"

"No, no boyfriend is pining away for me."

Jess giggled, she felt calm and confident enough to raise a subject that had been bothering her. "Look, I just want to sleep in the single bed. I think we'd both be more comfortable that way?"

"Of course."

Surely he didn't have to sound quite so happy about it. "So, how do I put it up?"

"Not a clue. The instructions must be in the manual somewhere." He performed contortions to get under the table, and lifted the floor panel to reveal a storage compartment full of leaflets and maps.

When Jess emerged from the bathroom in her pyjamas the table had been disconnected from the wall and cushions removed from the bench seat, but there was nothing resembling a bed.

"This make any sense to you?" he asked giving her the instruction book.

The diagram didn't look much like the van they were in, even allowing for it being of a left-hand drive model. "No, it doesn't."

They tried to move the seat and table into a position which matched the diagram, but it was incredibly awkward in the cramped space and they made no progress.

"Jess, we're both tired and I don't think these are the right instructions."

"Yes, I know. I suppose one more night won't make any difference, but promise we'll sort it out tomorrow?"

"I promise to try. I'm not sure we'll have any luck," he said as her put the table back in place.

He couldn't really say fairer than that, could he? It seemed she'd have to spend the rest of the trip sleeping in his bed. On the plus side she must be getting good at not complaining and trying to see the positives in any situation, because it didn't seem too much of a hardship. Tanya would be proud of her positive attitude.

Jess stifled a laugh as she shook out her sleeping bag and crawled into it. Christina wouldn't be impressed by that bit. Jess still had the smile on her face when, a little later, Eliot had finished in the bathroom and climbed over her to get into bed.

"OK?" he asked.

"Yes. Well, I'm a bit hot in this sleeping bag," she said quite truthfully. The first two nights it had seemed cosy, but the day's sunshine had warmed the interior of the van considerably.

"I'm not surprised. You could always get out of it, if you start to simmer."

Jess waited until he seemed to be asleep before wriggling free. It didn't help all that much. Technically she must be cooler, but her proximity to Eliot made her feel distinctly hot. She really, really shouldn't have thought about the advice Christina might give her, as now the sensible part of her brain which knew that putting it into action would be a bad idea, had gone to sleep. It took a long time for the rest of her to follow.

When she awoke, his arms were around her. Jess opened her eyes to see him smiling at her.

"Good morning," he whispered in a husky voice.

"Morning," she mumbled. "What's the time? I'd better get up."

"There's no rush."

Warm and comfortable though it was to lie in Eliot's arms and tempting though it was to stay there, Jess dragged herself out of bed. She heard the water heater cut in. That meant he'd turned it on long enough ago for it to heat, and then cool again. How long had he been holding her, watching her sleep?

She showered quickly then realised she had again forgotten about her clothes and had to come out in her towel to fetch them. This time she didn't have to watch him going through her underwear – he'd already laid some, and a short sleeved blouse and her loose flannel shorts, on the bed.

"Pink, I thought today," he said. A wicked smile played

on his lips.

She felt a blush rise up her chest and face. Marvellous, now her complexion matched the fuchsia pink shorts and balcony bra.

Jess made bacon and mushroom omelette for their breakfast, cooking it well so the eggs were set firm and the outside deliciously crisp and golden. She had everything ready by the time Eliot was washed, shaved and dressed. They chatted over the meal and discussed the day's plan.

"There's a river inlet I've heard about that I'd like to get some shots of. I think you'll like it – there should be plenty of different conditions and ways of looking at things."

"Sounds good to me."

"Looks like it's going to be a hot day. How about we take a picnic with us and walk?"

"OK… as long as it's not thirty miles each way."

"Not quite that far. It will be a fair trek though, so we'd better not carry more than we'll need."

Jess made up a salad and packed cheese, fruit and yoghurt. "What shall we take to drink?" she asked. He'd mentioned a picnic as though it was to be a pleasant event rather than wolfing down sandwiches between jobs. She didn't want to take wine assuming it was to be a relaxed day only to find he'd intended to work hard all day.

Eliot was staring at his laptop and didn't seem to have heard.

"What will you want to drink?" she repeated.

"Anything, doesn't matter." He wasn't happy.

"What's up?"

"I've had an order from your father."

Chapter 13

"What do you mean?" Jess asked. If Daddy wanted to cut the trip short, or divert them to another task, she'd refuse to go along with it.

Eliot showed her an email from Daddy's PA.

Mr Beatty,

My employer, Mr Borlase, is aware that on Friday you will be photographing those people who helped with the various conservation projects you are documenting. He is offering to pay for a portrait of everyone involved who'd like one. He requests that Jessica takes these portraits – under your direction, naturally.

As a token of his gratitude, Mr Borlase wishes to make a donation towards the refurbishment of the community centre, which he understands is in urgent need of attention.

Kind regards,

John Pardoe.

"How's that an order?" Jess asked.

"No, perhaps order isn't quite the right word."

"He's being nice, isn't he?"

"Hmm."

"Come on, tell me what you mean."

"It's blackmail, Jessica. I'm to run along and teach you how to take portraits and I get to look generous by offering them all a nice printed copy. Don't do it and all these good people lose the funding for the community centre they need and deserve. I don't doubt he's made the enquiries in such a way as to raise their hopes."

"I don't think that's quite fair…"

"No? He usually goes about things in a more straightforward manner, does he? Wouldn't invite me to dinner, offer funding for a project he knows is important to me, and then announce I've got a new assistant?"

"You're right, he shouldn't have treated you like that, but it's how he gets results in business."

"This isn't business. Or rather it's not his business. I don't like being manipulated. You're not business either. Don't you resent being part of one of his schemes?"

"I'm not! It's you who's being manipulated, not me."

"Oh really? You were uncomfortable, I could tell, when he announced you were coming on this trip without consulting either of us."

She couldn't meet his gaze, nor could she reply without being disloyal to her father.

"You didn't think to stand up to him and refuse?"

"I wanted you to teach me." She didn't like admitting she'd willingly become a party to the manipulation, even though she'd been unaware of it beforehand.

"I said I'd do that when I got back."

He had, but she'd been impatient to start and liked the idea of being in a confined space with him for days on end. He'd seemed not to really mind the idea on the evening he'd come round to her flat. Even when he'd picked her up and driven her to Wales he'd seemed happy enough. He'd stopped when she'd liked the view, just because she'd wanted to take photos. It wasn't until later he'd seemed annoyed with her. Had she done something wrong, made him feel manipulated? She didn't think so, but she realised John Pardoe's email certainly would seem that way.

"Eliot, I think this might be my fault. I emailed Daddy yesterday. I didn't ask him to do this, but I can see he might have thought it was something I'd want."

"And, of course, if Pumpkin wants to do something, then Daddy makes it happen?" He didn't sound angry.

Jess nodded. "Funny, I wasn't spoilt as a child. I did have a privileged life, but I wasn't simply bought anything I took a fancy to, even though I'm sure my parents could have afforded to do that, but since Mum got ill… I suppose he didn't know how else to try and comfort me and he sort of got in the habit." She stopped trying to explain. Why the situation arose wasn't as important as what she now did about it.

"You're right, Eliot. You were made to do this and I'm sorry for any part I had in that. I suppose I'm too used to getting what I want when I want it. I'm privileged and indulged, but I'm not a bad person."

"No, you're not. I'm not either really, just grumpy."

"Can we try to be friends?"

"Of course."

She'd offered her hand for him to shake, but he ignored it and gave her a hug. That was much more like it.

"So, what are we going to do about the portraits? Tell Daddy 'No'?"

"Up to you. Do you want to take them?"

"I would like to have a go. That's if you don't mind helping me, and if we've got time."

"I expect we can do something."

"Thanks, Eliot."

"How's that picnic coming along?"

"I was wondering what we should take to drink."

"Bottle of wine? I've been working you hard, we could take it a bit easier today." He even suggested going without the tripods to save carrying them.

Leaving the bag for litter behind obviously wasn't an option and when Jess saw how much fishing line, sometimes complete with hooks, they collected she was glad they had it. Who knew how many waterbirds, perhaps even otters, they were saving with that simple task.

The walk was every bit as varied as Eliot had suggested. The river meandered and at every twist and turn there was something new and beautiful to photograph. Shady fern covered banks gave way to open water meadows, which in turn were replaced by dramatic exposed rocks. At one point, where the riverbed widened out, they saw the remains of an old wrecked boat. It seemed to be melting into the gravel and its dark, decaying almost melancholic form contrasted wonderfully with the sunlight sparkling on the rippling water.

Eliot pointed out a piece of litter ahead of them. Jess had seen it too and would have picked it up when she reached the spot, but as she went to remove it for Eliot, she realised how the artificially brilliant white and electric blue crisp packet would have drawn attention in the photo and spoiled the shot. He could have removed it digitally, but had explained it was always better to take a perfect shot, if you could, than to try to fix something later. It seemed that litter picking might be playing a large part in her future.

After Eliot had taken a couple of shots, he said, "I shouldn't have let you off carrying the tripod."

"Can you rest the camera on that rock?"

"I could, but you haven't brought my beanbag either and I need something soft to rest the camera on. Your shorts will do."

"You're kidding!"

"Nope. That blouse has buttons on, so it's no good. Those shorts will be perfect."

She was so certain he didn't really expect her to undress for him that she called his bluff by hooking her thumbs into the waistband and tugging them down half an inch. His expression proved her right.

"I've got a better idea." Jess stepped right up to him and tugged at his T-shirt, exposing his flat stomach. It took time to wriggle the T-shirt free of his broad shoulders and strong arms. The fact he still had hold of the camera didn't help.

Once Eliot was topless, Jess paid even closer attention to the way he positioned his body to take the photos. With difficulty, she resisted running a hand over his tanned skin to feel exactly which muscles were tensed with the effort of keeping him perfectly still.

Eventually he gave her his camera to hold as he replaced his T-shirt. They walked on and Eliot chatted about the different shots he was taking and advised her when she wanted to get a particular effect.

They sat close together on a fallen tree for their picnic. Once they'd finished the pastrami salad, Eliot peeled an orange for her. Jess knew she'd always think of this day beside the river, and him, whenever she smelled orange zest.

He poured more wine. "So, why is there no boyfriend?" he asked.

"There have been some, but…" Jess explained about her mum being ill just as she was old enough for boyfriends. She'd helped nurse her at home because they didn't want her to go into a hospice. Jess's voice cracked and hot tears ran down her face. She'd never be able to tell Mum that she was in love or take a man home to meet her. Daddy would care, but not in the same way.

Eliot put his arms around her and held her until she stopped crying. He wiped away her tears with his thumb. "Oh, Jess."

Poor man, he'd only asked a simple question. Jess took a few deep breaths and made herself smile. "Sorry, I hardly ever cry. I'm not sure what came over me. Drinking in the middle of the day perhaps."

"It must have been a very difficult time, I'm not surprised it still upsets you to think about it."

"I try not to, think about it, I mean. Anything that reminds me or Dad of Mum's illness has gone. There are no pictures of her when she was sick, we don't talk about it and I don't eat white foods."

"Hmm. What is it with that?"

"The chemo made her scared to eat anything that wasn't totally bland, so it was just plain white bread, boiled white fish, mashed potatoes. We all had the same as even smelling other foods made her nauseous."

"You could have eaten somewhere else."

"That's what she said, and I did sometimes, but then I felt guilty."

"Your father didn't want you eating normal food?"

"He didn't ever tell me not to…"

"No, he wouldn't need to."

Jess didn't want to get into another argument about

Daddy with Eliot. He might think he'd been a little hard on his daughter, but it was only because he'd loved his wife so much and was so upset that he was losing her. Since then he'd done his best to make up to Jess for his neglect at that time and she'd been the whole focus of his attention whenever he wasn't working. At least she had until he'd met Lizzie. Jess realised that despite wanting a let-up from her father's almost obsessive care of her, she'd still resented Lizzie for her part in producing that relief. Jess didn't want to think about that either.

"Anyway, I was very awkward with boys when I'd stopped grieving. In a lot of ways I was young for my age."

"So you avoided men?"

"No, not avoided, but something always seemed to go wrong. A boyfriend once got caught trying to climb in through my bedroom window. Daddy sorted him out and made sure he didn't work in the Post Office after that, so it was OK, but the police told him not to do anything like that again."

"Sorted him out?" Why did Eliot look so surprised? It was almost as though he thought she'd meant it in the mafia sense. No; it wasn't possible for anyone to imagine Daddy doing anything so awful.

"Of course. He wants to help whenever he can."

Poor Phil! He'd been out for a jog, noticed her light on and asked if he could come up. He'd got stuck in the tiny decorative balcony and Jess had been laughing too much to help. Unfortunately a police officer spotted his tracksuit and trainers and assumed it was an attempted robbery.

Daddy wasn't pleased to be woken up, but eventually saw the funny side. When he'd discovered Phil was a talented badminton player, he'd given him a job at part-time hours on full time pay, so he no longer needed to work on his fitness at night. The employment had lasted much longer than the relationship between Jess and Phil.

"Who exactly was he trying to help?"

"I'm sure he did what he thought was best for everyone. Afterwards he introduced me to men he thought would be suitable. He'd like me happily married and producing grandchildren, but they all seemed far more interested in what Daddy could do for them than in me."

"You're being a bit hard on yourself, Jess. Why wouldn't a man be interested in you?"

She could have asked why he wasn't. She thought better of it. It did seem he was starting to like her as a friend, perhaps even assistant, and she didn't want to be told it would never be more than that.

"I don't know how to attract a man," she confessed.

"You don't have to do anything, just be yourself."

"That's not working too well."

"I think that's because you don't really know who you are. You've been rather in your father's shadow, haven't you?"

"Daddy's been very good to me."

"I know, it wasn't really supposed to be a criticism. He cares for you and wants the best, but if you don't do something about it you'll find yourself married to a man your father has chosen and living in a house he's provided and wondering what your life could have been like if you'd taken a few risks."

Jess nodded. That was pretty much how she'd felt before she'd taken the college course. She'd been working for Daddy, mixing with people Daddy introduced her to, living in Daddy's home. No wonder people only saw her in terms of her relationship to her father. Eliot was right, she had to break free. The next time a risk appealed to her, she would take it. She looked up to see Eliot's mouth just inches from hers and was tempted to kiss him.

"OK, I'll see if I can find the real me and if I do, I'll let her take a few brave steps away from Daddy's side." Jess leant forward and kissed his cheek. It was a very small step, but nothing bad happened.

He seemed slightly amused, but definitely not horrified or angry. "Good. I'm looking forward to seeing the real Jess in action."

"The real me wants to take more pictures."

"Then she shall."

They packed up, ready to move on.

As they'd walked, she'd loved the way the trees framed the view, but been irritated that each time the scene ahead was especially attractive, there weren't any convenient branches hanging low enough to be included.

"What's up?" he asked her when he spotted her standing on tiptoe, to try again.

When she explained, he leapt into the air, grabbed a slender branch and held onto it, bringing it lower. "Better?"

"Much, yes. Why didn't I think of just moving the tree?"

"Eliminatory beginner's mistake," he said shaking his head. "A bit like leaving your lens cap on."

She heard his bark of laughter almost before she'd tilted up her camera to check she hadn't really done anything so stupid. The new Jessica was not going to let him get away with that. She wasn't going to have a temper tantrum, but she'd think of something to even the score.

Chapter 14

The next morning Jess was wakened by Eliot blowing gently on her cheek. She turned toward him and her lips brushed against his.

"Time to get up, sleeping beauty. We're wasting daylight."

"It's still dark," she mumbled. And maybe she was still asleep? His attitude to her seemed to have changed so rapidly that parts of it felt like a dream.

"Only just, come on." He pulled the quilt off her and scooped her into his arms. He held her for a brief moment before lifting her and swinging her legs over the edge of the bed and then releasing her so she slithered through his arms until her feet touched the floor.

She was glad she only had to take a few steps to reach the bathroom because she was shaking so much and her heart was pounding so hard she didn't think she'd have made it much further. It wasn't fair that he could have such an impact on her yet remain unaffected himself. Yesterday he'd comforted her when she was upset. Later that day he'd shown her what was meant by 'lead in lines' – using lines such as railings, railway tracks or ploughed furrows to draw the viewer's gaze toward the principle subject in an image. He'd been a patient and encouraging teacher, but training her was part of the deal. Was he only treating her differently because he'd realised she wasn't going to quit and he might as well make the most of having an assistant?

Jess braced herself for a nasty shock in the bathroom mirror, as for once it wasn't steamed up. She'd not used a face mask for days and the lack of time and suitable reflection to apply make-up meant she'd also skipped her usual cleansing and toning. As for her hair, it had received no attention other than a dab of hastily rinsed out conditioner and infrequent combings the entire trip. It should have been a horrible ball of frizz and her skin dull and lifeless but neither was true. Her complexion was clear and prettily blushed by exposure to the sun. Her long hair fell in healthy looking relaxed curls.

Why had she thought she needed all those expensive products and to waste time applying them and constantly straightening her hair? The answer came almost immediately – she'd had time to fill and nothing much other than herself to think about. However this trip turned out, the new Jess wouldn't be like that.

After a quick breakfast, they drove close to the location Eliot had selected for their next shoot. Jess eagerly pulled on her backpack, accepted his tripod and set off for her next lesson and next chance to impress Eliot with her usefulness and charming personality. As they climbed, they caught glimpses of the sea.

"What's that island?" Jess asked.

"I think it must be Skomer."

"Where the puffins are? I'd love to go."

"We can't, Jess."

"I know. It's a working trip."

"You could stay on afterwards," Eliot suggested. "Get that train home after all."

"Or you could stay on another day and we could both

go."

"Not possible. I have another job lined up straight after this."

Jess noticed he'd only said that he couldn't, not that he didn't want to. Maybe it was something they could do together in the future.

The sun was up by then and the ruined building ahead was bathed in a warm, rich light. She wondered who had lived there and what their lives had been like.

"What was this, a castle?" she asked.

"Maybe, or perhaps a look-out post. I don't really know, to be honest."

She wanted to get the sense it wasn't just a defensive position, but had been a home, or at least a place where real people had lived or worked. Even if it had only been occupied by soldiers, they must have eaten, talked, maybe laughed and joked with each other. When Eliot had taken the pictures he wanted, in the best of the early light, she tried to explain this to him.

"You going all romantic on me?" he asked.

"What if I am?" she challenged. "Isn't it a good thing that we look at things in a different way, for work I mean." She didn't want to imply she had anything against him developing romantic feelings. "I'll take my own pictures that way, not just copies of yours."

"Go on then, see what you can do."

He sat on the grass and watched as she walked all around the ruin looking for signs of the people who'd once been there. There was a whole window space still complete and she used that to, she hoped, draw the eye inside the remains of the building. If properly cropped the image should be interesting, but Jess doubted it would create the effect she wanted. There wasn't enough building left to give the feel of someone looking in at a safe haven. She couldn't find anything which suggested the original occupants, but there was plenty of evidence of later visitors. Unfortunately litter played a part. Jess gathered that up to take away with her.

"What is wrong with people?" she asked. "They come out here to appreciate the beauty of the place or look at the birds and then they spoil it."

"You're giving people too much credit, I suspect. This is probably a spot for couples to meet."

He was right. One of the items Jess picked up was a used condom. She used a discarded crisp bag as a temporary glove to collect it. Thankfully the user had partially stuffed it back into the empty packet. That just annoyed her all the more. If they'd taken the trouble to put it in the pack, how much harder could it have been to take it home?

"That's no excuse. Why would you want to spoil a place that you associate with love?" she asked.

"I wouldn't, but not everyone is like us, Jess." She had the feeling he wanted to say more, but thought better of it.

Jess spotted initials which had long ago been carved into one of the crumbling beams. An A and an S with a heart between them. Alan and Suzy? Anne and Simon? She decided to think of them as Alan and Suzy as she liked the idea the boy had done this to show his love for the girl. He'd have worked with her watching, or perhaps come up earlier and done it, then brought her to see. The girl, Suzy, would have been so happy to know he loved her for herself and they'd have kissed. Maybe later they'd come here for him to propose, stopped off after their wedding to have photographs taken, this really was a wonderful spot for that, with the backdrop of the sea crashing against the strong rocks… She laughed then, amused at the way her imagination was running away with her. Good thing Eliot couldn't read her mind or he really would tease her about being romantic.

When she looked across at him he was pacing about and had his arm up as though talking on his phone. Perhaps she was mistaken though as when he saw her, he waved and then pushed both hands into his pockets. Jess thought it unlikely he'd have got a signal, but hadn't brought her own phone for that reason, so couldn't check.

Jess photographed the carved initials. She liked the image, but it was a little too stark for the romantic image she wanted. It was a shame the beam wasn't lower so she could include some grass or even wild flowers. She remembered Eliot pulling down a branch for her. She wouldn't ask him to pick flowers for her, but Alan could gather some for Suzy.

Although she was careful to select only common varieties; tufted vetch, scabious, pink campion and sea thrift, which were plentiful in the area, it didn't take long to pick a few pretty flowers. Piling up rocks to put them on was much more time consuming. Next she built a framework of grass, heather and sticks to support her flowers so they'd look as though they were growing.

"OK, there?" Eliot called.

"Patience. Romance can't be rushed."

Taking the picture didn't take long at all, but when she looked back Eliot was laid flat as though asleep. She grinned as an idea formed in her mind. First she climbed up on some fallen stones to check her plan would work, then she walked quietly back to where Eliot was snoring loudly and unconvincingly.

"Are you asleep?"

"Yes."

"You won't notice this then," she bent down and tucked the flowers into his hand.

Other than slightly opening one eye, he didn't react. She walked back and took a picture through the window, using it to frame the image of a sleeping Eliot clutching the flowers. To her he looked just like a handsome hero waiting to present his love with the blooms.

By the time she'd walked back to him he was sitting up, the flowers nowhere to be seen.

"Ready?"

"Yes."

"Come on then, we've got a lot to do today."

"Oh sorry, I didn't realise…" She'd been messing about for ages on a whim and held him up.

"It's all right, Jess. I'm not blaming you, I've only just noticed the time."

As they walked back to the van, Eliot said, "You like puffins?"

"Adore them! They're so cute. Their little faces and that funny way they walk. You probably think it's cheesy, but I'd love to get a shot of one with its beak full of sand eels."

"And want to go over to Skomer?"

Hadn't he just said it wasn't possible? Wondering if this was some kind of test, she kept her voice as casual as possible. "Do we have time for that?"

"No. But if we work really hard for ridiculously long hours, then we could probably make time."

"Not take it easy like we have been up to now?"

"No. It's no fun if it's too easy! It'll be tough, Jess, but if you want to, and the weather holds, we'll hope to get everything done in time for a few hours puffin watching next Thursday."

There might not be room to show her feelings in the van, but they were outside on a Welsh hill. Jess flung her arms round Eliot and kissed him.

"Behave yourself, woman," he said, but he was smiling.

It was probably just as well she'd be working to the point of exhaustion. That was the only way she'd be able to sleep next to a man she really liked, wanted even more, but wasn't allowed to touch.

They worked hard for the rest of the day, walking miles and carrying lots of equipment. Whilst driving to one shoot she said, "You're a great teacher, Eliot. I'm really improving."

"Yeah." He sounded wary again.

"I'd like to keep copies of some of the pictures I've taken, if that's all right."

"Of course it is. If you take a photo then you own the copyright until you give it away or sell it."

"Oh, OK."

"What's up? You don't seem happy about that."

"I just thought… it doesn't matter."

He pulled over and switched off the engine.

"It matters if you're not happy. Come on, tell me what's up."

"I was thinking you might want to use some of the ones I'd taken. Sorry, that's silly, of course you wouldn't."

"I might do, I can't say until I have all the material together."

She nodded, that was entirely reasonable.

"That's why I had you sign the form to allow me to do that, but they'd still be your pictures. I'd credit you for any I used and I wouldn't take your copyright away. That's not fair."

"OK, thanks."

"Talking of paperwork, I'm planning to use those model release forms of yours in future, if you don't mind?"

"Of course not."

"Usually I don't bother as the few times I photograph people, it's either at their request, or the purpose is clear, but having it in writing is sensible."

"I'm glad to be of some use."

He was being nice to cheer her up, but that didn't stop her feeling stupid for thinking he'd want to use any of her pictures when he'd taken so many excellent ones himself.

"You all right, really?" Eliot asked.

"Yes. Come on, let's go or we'll be eating at midnight."

As they spent the afternoon and evening photographing recently restored woodland around a stately home, Jess thought about why she'd been so upset. It wasn't because she thought no one would see her pictures and she'd been wasting her time. As she'd told him, she'd learnt a lot and knew her work was much improved. She was unhappy because Eliot didn't need her, not as a photographer nor in any other way.

Could he ever want her? She didn't feel she knew him well enough to guess. In fact she knew very little about him, far less than he knew about her. He'd seemed to know a lot about her life from when Mummy was ill and the way her grief had affected future relationships and even her eating habits. Usually she kept such things to herself. She'd been more open with Eliot than with anyone else, but it had felt like explaining to someone who already knew more than the bare facts of her mother's death. How could he know how much her illness still affected Jess? She'd kept most of it hidden even from Zoe, Alyssa and Christina.

On Friday, Jess and Eliot returned to the beach where they'd previously met Llewellyn, the volunteer co-ordinator who'd mistakenly referred to Jess as Eliot's girlfriend. The last of the morning light was used to photograph seabirds, now able to walk and feed without the risk of getting trapped in plastic bags and fishing line.

When Llewellyn arrived he greeted them both warmly. "Thank you so much for the donation towards our community centre. It will make a huge difference to several local organisations."

"Nothing to do with me," Eliot said.

"I'll pass your thanks on to the board of Borlase Marketing," Jess said. Llewellyn didn't need to know she was thirty per cent of that board and her father the remainder.

"Oh, I thought…"

Jess continued, "The company are sponsoring another conservation project which we'll be photographing later in the year and when they heard about all the work you've done here, wanted to make a contribution."

"Oh, I see."

Jess wasn't sure he did and took care to only introduce herself using her first name to the volunteers who'd come to pose for photographs.

Eliot had already explained he wanted a mix of formal

and informal group photos to use for publicity and possibly in his exhibition. In addition to this she was to take the individual portraits her father was paying for.

"I will be taking some myself," Eliot said. "They'll expect that, but treat this as your assignment. If you're photographing an event there are likely to be other photographers covering it. You need to get everything you want, no matter what they're doing."

Llewellyn and his friends were happy to sign Jess's model release forms. They joked about and teased each other, and Jess, as Eliot helped her to direct them for the shots, and they both took photographs.

At one point as Eliot was advising Jess on the correct settings to use, someone called out, "Don't forget to take your lens cap off!"

Thanks to Eliot saying the same thing not so long ago, Jess was spared the embarrassment of checking in front of a large group. That didn't mean he was quite forgiven for laughing at her though.

Chapter 15

Jess and Eliot took portraits of groups of people who'd helped with restoration or ecological work in various ways; Girl Guides, local tradespeople, various clubs and groups of friends who'd spent a great many hours over the previous year collecting litter and clearing overgrown paths, and those who'd provided much needed refreshments.

Jess saw what Eliot had meant about working around another photographer. When he'd arranged a group to his liking, she photographed them too from a different angle. If she'd waited until he'd finished she'd have wasted everyone's time and quite likely lost some of their goodwill.

Eliot flirted outrageously with the Guide leader who was about ninety-three, and joked with the girls, making everyone giggle. He paid no attention to Jess as she took her pictures. She was a little hurt by that, especially as the girls ignored her too. It did enable her to take some lovely candid shots, but she felt she was being sidelined on what was supposed to be her assignment.

She could probably have won the Guides over by buying chocolate and crisps claiming it was so the wrappers could be used as litter props, but that would have fed her ego at the expense of getting the job done in a reasonable amount of time.

"I'll take some formal portraits now," Jess announced.

Eliot helped her get the girls to pose as Jess wanted them. They, and he, did their best, but the adolescents were terribly self-conscious the moment they realised the camera was pointed at them while all their friends looked on.

Jess beckoned Eliot to her side and said, "These are going to be awful; like the most staged and boring school photos."

"Try telling a joke," Eliot suggested. "Or take a few pictures, pretend you've finished and grab a couple more once they've relaxed."

Every joke she'd ever heard, except a few of Christina's very worst, immediately deleted themselves from Jess's memory. Those she did recall, whilst not suitable for the Guides, did at least distract Jess from the pressure of the task. She found that once she was relaxed it was easier to talk to the girls and take their minds off what she was doing.

Another group of photographic subjects were the men who'd spent a weekend repairing the crumbling sea wall. Jess snapped informal shots of everyone as they clustered around Eliot telling him of their contribution. It struck her that there had been a lot more difficulty in getting permission to do the work than in actually completing it. The men seemed very pleased with themselves and wanted to be sure their names were spelled correctly in any resulting publications.

Jess didn't have any trouble getting them to pose or smile as they all wanted to preen in front of her. She was starting to get weary of their smug faces and knew the pictures were likely to reflect her lack of interest.

"How about we take some by the wall? Show the result of your efforts?" she said.

"Not just a pretty face, are you?" one said as they eagerly set off to pose in the new location.

The men had done so little work that most of them could identify the few rocks or sleepers they'd helped put in place. They were happy to re-enact the scene by holding up the strapping they'd used to allow the digger to manoeuvre the heavy items into place.

"You used a digger?" she asked with surprise. From the fuss they'd made she'd assumed they'd moved the items with sheer muscle power.

"Gerard here is a JCB driver."

"Can you get the digger down here? That'd make a good picture," Jess said.

Gerard was pleased with that idea and set off to get his machine.

In the meantime, the man whom Jess mentally christened The Major, who'd co-ordinated that particular effort, suggested Jess come to his home so she could take shots of him at his computer, doing verbal battle with the council.

"Are they giving you trouble?" Eliot asked as they set off up the path.

"Nothing I can't handle."

"But?"

Jess hadn't wanted to moan, but perhaps telling him how she felt would make her feel better and therefore able to tackle the shots with more enthusiasm. "Unlike Llewellyn and his friends, this lot don't seem particularly interested in conservation, just in bragging about their efforts. They're making a lot of fuss but don't seem to have done very much."

"No, but they did do something. They gave up some of

their time and the wall is now safe."

Jess remembered Tanya's comment at the 'Before and After' exhibition; that for Jess doing something meant giving money. She'd made a donation there. On Capri she'd done the same for a wildlife charity, but hadn't even thought of giving up an afternoon, or even an hour, of sightseeing to help collect litter.

Her phone rang. The display showed it was her father calling. His interference was something she could take action on.

After exchanging greetings she said, "Daddy, you shouldn't have said anything about those portraits without speaking to me first."

"Pumpkin…"

She couldn't let him speak, or she'd end up telling him she appreciated his attempt to help and so invite him to do the same thing again. "Daddy, I've got less than a week of this trip left, could you please not interfere?"

"All right, Pumpkin." He sounded so sad.

"Thanks, Daddy. It's just that I want to do something for myself. I am looking forward to working with you, and Lizzie, on the Dibden Spit project."

"Now, don't you worry about that. It's all going to be fine." His tone was so much brighter that Jess was really glad she'd remembered Lizzie wanted to get involved in the project too. She assured her father she was well and happy, then ran after Eliot.

He'd reached The Major's impressive beachfront home before Jess caught up, so she missed her chance to tell Eliot he was right and she'd been too dismissive of the men's efforts.

The Major provided official looking letters for his

troops to pose with and staged a meeting in his conservatory. He read her a few extracts of messages from the council. "It'll give you a flavour of what we were up against and set the mood."

Jess almost giggled at his attention to detail – using method acting to pose for a simple picture. As she listened she gained more respect for the men. Fixing the path hadn't been of particular benefit to any of them. They all had cars and could easily drive past the place where the path had become unsafe. They had been thinking of the students who used that route as the quickest way between college, library and pubs. Of the mothers who walked along there to get to the shops, and holidaymakers, walkers and bird watchers.

Gerard was soon back with his digger and he was more than happy to position it so the JCB caught the light nicely. Jess didn't begrudge him trying to ensure the men posing in front didn't block the website address of his company painted on the outside. She knew her father did what amounted to the same thing whenever Borlase Marketing made charitable donations. No doubt the company name would show up prominently in connection with the Dibden Spit project.

Jess and Eliot took pictures of the wall itself and the views available to those who walked along it. As they did that, Jess saw the point of some of the earlier landscape pictures – they showed the areas which could now be accessed by walking along the coastal path. It seemed Eliot never took a picture without good purpose.

Once all the portraits had been taken, some volunteers asked if they could have pictures emailed to them. Jess almost told them there was no need as they'd all be receiving printed, framed copies. She glanced at Eliot and had the feeling he was ready to judge her response. "Will we be able to send email copies?"

He nodded. "But not immediately."

"We have Llewellyn's email address, so we'll forward everything to him," Jess said before The Major could offer himself as the point of contact. She had the feeling Eliot approved.

Eliot and Jess were again invited to the beach barbecue which was planned for Monday evening.

"I've arranged a hog roast," The Major told them.

"Would you like to go, Jess?" Eliot asked. Such a contrast to the way she'd tried to force him into accepting when they'd first been asked.

"Yes, it sounds great. Thank you so much for asking us."

"You can park your camper on my drive overnight, if you like. Plenty of room and as you've seen, it's not far to walk."

"That would be very convenient, thanks," Eliot said.

Jess was looking forward to coming back and joining the party. In some cases it had taken her a while to appreciate their good points, but Jess rather liked the volunteers. The thought of not having to cook dinner appealed too. She could almost taste the roasting pork and other succulent foods all delicately scented with wood smoke.

Eliot and Jess went back to the beach during golden hour, to take pictures when it was at its most beautiful. It was deserted. Had anyone seen them by the water's edge at sunset they'd probably have assumed they were lovers out for a romantic stroll. The way Eliot talked of nothing but apertures, composition and ISO settings rather spoiled that fantasy for Jess.

"This is a good spot," he said. "I'd like you to pose for a few shots, please."

"More of me?"

"Not you specifically. I want someone in silhouette to provide foreground interest."

"Oh, OK." She managed to sound as unenthusiastic as he'd done, even though she liked the idea of him having to pay some attention to her. As he worked she reflected on the way Eliot had ignored her earlier in the day and gradually realised it hadn't been a slight. By distracting the volunteers from her, they'd stopped thinking of themselves as models and Jess had been able to take natural looking photos. His infrequent advice, given quietly and phrased as suggestions, had helped her confidence too.

Actually he was helping her in all sorts of ways. Thanks to him, Jess felt she was at last starting to grow beyond the little girl living in Daddy's shadow. Could that be deliberate too and if so, did it mean he cared about her?

"Your romantic shots from yesterday have given me an idea," Eliot said. He set up a tripod and used the time delay so he could take shots of the two of them together. He got her into position, depressed the shutter then ran down to put his arm around her waist and pull her close.

"Don't move," he warned her.

Jess had no wish to move away from the warmth of his body and the delightful feeling of his arm on the thin material covering her back. All of her senses seemed heightened. Hearing the gentle lap of the sea, Eliot's steady breathing after running towards her, feeling the strength of the muscles of his legs and arm pressed close against her, the warmth of his body contrasted with the cool breeze, seeing the last fiery hues as the sun sunk lower, smelling Eliot's distinctive scent of skin and soap. She couldn't help wondering what he would taste like if he were to kiss her.

She heard the shutter click, but didn't try to move away. Neither did Eliot and she dared to hope he was actually enjoying holding her. The shutter clicked again.

"How many are you taking?" she asked.

"Five, I'm going to try an HDR shot."

"What's that?"

"Another thing you weren't taught on that course of yours?"

"Apparently so."

"High dynamic range. I'll take five images, some under and some over exposed and," he broke off as the shutter clicked for the fifth time. "Stay there, we'll have another one." He was soon back beside her, holding her close.

As they stood watching the sunset he promised to try to find the time to show her how the HDR process worked. Eliot took several more batches of pictures, even after it was so dark Jess couldn't imagine they'd be of any use. She didn't question him on the matter though. To do so might make him stop holding her. Perhaps he was using some special technique he assumed she'd know all about?

They hadn't had time for breakfast before setting out early that morning and lunch was coffee and chocolate biscuits shared with the volunteers, so by sunset they were both very hungry.

"We've got sausages, how about having them with mash

and beans?" Eliot suggested. "I can probably manage that if you want to download the pictures."

Jess tried not to show her horror at the thought of mashed potatoes. It was mostly because of her father's portrait 'commission' and partly because of her wish to see puffins, they'd had such a rushed day, so she didn't want to make a fuss. She could, however, make a different meal.

"How about a croque-monsieur? That's quick and easy."

"A crock what?"

"It's a kind of fried cheese and ham sandwich."

"Sounds good to me, but I might need some instruction."

"Oh. Yes." The thought of a mound of pale, bland, easy to digest potato had stopped her realising that he'd offered to swap their usual roles.

"Crack a couple of eggs into a… anything that's big enough to lay a sandwich in."

Following her instructions, Eliot had soon beaten the eggs, assembled the sandwiches and fried them to a delicious golden brown. By the time the food was ready, Jess had downloaded the pictures, deleted the obvious duds (all hers) keyworded and filed the images. When she came across the one she'd taken of him holding her flowers, Jess hesitated over leaving it on his hard drive, but decided not to delete it.

"Grub's up," Eliot said. "Leave those until after we've eaten, then I'll show you what to do next, OK?"

"Best sandwich ever," Eliot declared after making short work of his. "Thanks for teaching me the recipe." He moved round to sit next to Jess.

She did her best to concentrate on what he was doing to the photos, but her attention was mainly on the pleasure of having him so close with his arm around her shoulder. She watched his fingers on the keyboard and wondered what it would feel like if he were to dance them gently over her skin instead. The campervan was warm, she'd eaten a heavy meal and she was very tired. Soon she was drifting off to sleep, leaning against him.

"Bed for you, my girl," he declared.

Jess staggered into the bathroom and then hauled herself up onto the bed. She must have dozed off as he brushed his teeth, because it seemed Eliot immediately climbed in behind her. She pulled in her legs so he could get past.

When she stretched out flat on the bed it felt as though something was missing. She was cold, the warmth of Eliot's body was what was missing. Just minutes ago they'd been snuggled up together on the bench seat, now there was a space between them. Jess rolled over to be close to him.

Chapter 16

Jess didn't remember anything after that until Eliot gently shook her early the next morning.

"Wakey wakey."

She stumbled out the shower and took the mug of coffee he offered. Again it felt like she was being woken in the middle of the night, but Eliot was already shaved and dressed so to him it must seem that he'd let her sleep in. She could probably learn to get used to early starts, but not if they were all preceded by sunset photography.

They drove to yet another new location to take pictures in the morning light. The scenery was beautiful, but Jess started to wish it wasn't. If Wales had been flat and dull then she could have stayed in bed. She was tired, but she couldn't convince even herself that her aching limbs and heavy eyes were the main reason she wished she could be back under the duvet, snuggling up to Eliot. Although she needed all the sleep she was getting it didn't seem quite fair that she fell asleep immediately and missed feeling him close to her.

This time they'd had breakfast, but she was really hungry when they finished the shoot just after two.

"Let's buy something ready-made for lunch and something to take for this barbecue on Monday," Eliot said.

"OK. What should we take? I've never been to a barbecue before."

"You're kidding me?"

"No, why would I? I do know what one is, but I don't know what guests would be expected to take. Presumably we don't all turn up with a pound of sausages?"

Eliot laughed. "No, the food will be provided, we just need a bottle of wine or some beer. People usually bring whatever they like to drink, although there's no guarantee that won't get drunk by someone else."

Jess chose a bottle of wine. "Maybe I should get more than one and keep hold of the second so I've got something decent to drink?"

"I like your thinking."

"I want to get a few bottles of nice soft drinks too, for the Girl Guides. I went to lots of parties with my parents when I was little. While everyone else had champagne and cocktails I was given a choice of mineral water or coffee."

"If you really want to make the Guides happy, buy chocolate biscuits and marshmallows."

"Wouldn't they rather have a tin of Quality Street or something like that?"

"Trust me."

She bought the things he'd suggested, but as they drove back, asked, "How do you know so much about what Girl Guides like? And don't tell me you were one."

"I wasn't, but Lizzie was."

"Lizzie? Oh yes, you were friends as children, weren't you?" She tried to sound casual.

"Sort of. I've known her since I was a baby. Our mothers job-shared and also shared looking after us during working hours. Lizzie is six years older than me and I hero-worshipped her back then."

How did he feel now? Jess chided herself for

entertaining a twinge of jealous ill will towards the woman who was engaged to her father. Jess was certain that although Lizzie might appreciate his wealth and social standing, she did genuinely care about Daddy.

"There's a six year age gap between us too, isn't there?" Eliot asked.

"There is, but don't go thinking I hero-worship you."

"I don't think; I know!"

Thankfully they were back 'home' in their field by then, so Jess was spared having to deny that.

As Jess made a pot of tea, Eliot said, "I'm going to impress you even more now by showing you the advantages of HDR." As he brought up five images taken inside a church they'd photographed earlier in the week, he explained that by combining over and under exposed images he could capture all the details in the shadows without burning out highlights in the better lit areas.

"That sounds great in theory," Jess said. "But I think sometimes it's good to have mysterious shadows or areas so light you can feel the sun streaming in."

"OK, so which of these five would you choose?" he asked her.

She looked through. One had caught every beautiful detail in the stained glass windows, but was dark everywhere else. The one at the opposite extreme showed the carved wood gently gleaming where generations of hands had polished it smooth. The windows, however, were just white spaces. In every image something was lost while something else was gained.

"I suppose it would have to be the middle one. That's probably how I'd have taken it. Or at least tried to," she amended her statement at the end, aware these were Eliot's pictures and that she'd taken her own which he'd not shown her yet.

"Let's see yours, then," he brought forward her laptop and found the appropriate image. It was very like the one she'd selected from his, except that she'd taken it at a slightly different angle so the brightest window wasn't included.

"Yes, that's good. I'd say it was better than that at the moment," he indicated his own 'middle' picture. "You've avoided shooting the window which would have been most over exposed, so the brightness is better balanced and you've not lost too much detail."

"I think I'd have been pleased with this if I hadn't seen the others and realised I was missing stuff."

"You should be pleased, you've made a good job of making the best of the situation. How would this have looked if you'd taken it a few weeks ago?"

Jess was able to show him, as she'd taken some pictures inside another church on Capri. She scrolled through them.

"They're pretty bad, aren't they?" she said, almost to herself.

He didn't have to answer. Most had both burnt out highlights and missing detail in the shadows as well as being poorly framed and in a couple of cases they weren't even properly in focus.

"Delete them," she said.

"No, you do it later, but not until you've looked through again and worked out where you went wrong. Do that and these aren't wasted."

Eliot began processing his combined image. Soon he had every detail perfectly clear. She could see every rich colour in the window and the stitching of the prayer kneeling cushions in the darkest spots under pews.

"It is better, but…"

"But what?" His tone wasn't defensive.

"It doesn't look quite real. It's more like a painting. Perhaps it's because I know that you couldn't photograph it like that."

"But I have."

"Yes, sort of. Sorry, I didn't mean to criticise. This is very clever and…"

"Explain what you mean." He spoke gently, as though really interested in her opinion.

"If it was for a text book or something where you had to show as much detail as possible in one picture, it would be perfect, but to show what the place is really like it's, well, too perfect. When I was there I couldn't see it like that. When I looked toward the window I was too dazzled to see into the shadows."

"I agree. Sometimes too perfect doesn't work. If you looked at this without seeing how it was done then I think you'd still have realised it wasn't right without knowing why. What you said about mysterious shadows and the sun streaming in was exactly right."

Eliot adjusted the image so the centre of the brightest window was very slightly burnt out and a little of the detail was lost in the darkest area.

"That's it, perfect!"

Eliot went through some of the pictures she'd taken and showed her more techniques for processing and improving them. She really tried to concentrate on what he was saying and doing, but was again distracted by having him so close. She was also thinking how good it felt to not have to walk, stand or carry anything. At least it did until they went to refill the van with fresh water.

"We'll have a go at night shots this evening," Eliot said as the last canister of water glugged through the funnel into the van's tank. He explained these actually had to be taken at dusk, not in complete darkness, which was a relief. She doubted she'd have stayed awake long enough for that. As it was, she was fairly sure the ones she took were rubbish. Eliot had told her she'd need to use a tripod, but that was something she'd never attempted and her tired brain wouldn't take in the instructions he tried to give her.

"Is it dark enough?" she asked as the sun sunk out of sight.

"Not quite. We're aiming for the sky in the finished image to be the same shade as the delightful dress you had on the night your father came up with the interesting idea of us taking this trip together."

Jess could remember exactly how he'd looked that evening, but had no idea what she'd been wearing. Was his eye for detail coupled with a photographic memory, or had she made the kind of impression which stuck in his mind?

Although she'd been mentally meal planning as she shopped, Jess simply couldn't think of anything exciting she could make for dinner with the food in the fridge, so decided to cook the sausage, beans and mash Eliot had requested the night before. She peeled just enough potatoes for Eliot as she didn't intend eating any herself.

"You'll need more than that, I'm famished," he said and took another from the bag. Then another. "There's only one more, you might as well use the lot."

Too tired to argue, she peeled them all.

Instead of closing the laptop and moving it away when Jess tried to serve the food, he just slid it into the corner, turned toward her.

"These are no good." He still spoke gently, but as she could see he was right, that did little to soften the criticism.

She was trying so hard, but just couldn't cope with all the work, learning new skills and adjusting to living conditions which were hardly luxurious, without making a few mistakes. At times it felt as though she only kept going because she couldn't summon the strength to walk away. It wasn't just physical strength she lacked; leaving Eliot, losing the little of his respect she'd gained, possibly never to see him again, would be impossible.

Next Eliot showed her a couple more of the night shots she'd just taken. The sky on the screen was a rich shade of cobalt blue, one of her favourite colours. That was the only good thing about them. "See, they're not sharp at all," he said.

"I'm not surprised. Some of the time I'm too tired to think straight. That's not supposed to be a whinge. I guess I'm far more used to an easy life and having things done for me than I realised."

"If I slacken the pace, then we won't get so much done. I wouldn't take all the shots I wanted, which would be a disadvantage for me, but I wouldn't be being fair to you either. The more shoots we do in the biggest range of conditions, the more you'll learn. If you want to be professional, you can't just choose to work on nice sunny days and you can't make time stand still."

Jess dolloped mash and beans onto the plates as she listened to his explanations. He was right – as usual. He'd said the trip would be too much for her and she'd proved it by sleepwalking through his most recent lessons.

"You need to know how to work under pressure, time,

weather…" He paused until Jess looked up from serving their food, and smiled at her. "Even coping with a really grumpy client."

She bit back the sharp remark which sprang to mind and managed a return smile. "Yeah, you're giving me top training for that one!"

"And there's the puffins."

She'd almost forgotten he'd offered to take her to Skomer if they worked ridiculously hard. Jess knew she'd forget her exhaustion if she was able to get a close view of a puffin. She sat opposite Eliot, staring at the screen, half listening to his critique and forking food into her mouth. The quicker she ate, the quicker she could sleep. Luckily, apart from the sausages, it didn't need any chewing.

When she'd almost finished dinner Eliot showed her some examples of the portraits she'd taken. She could see they were good. Far, far better than the snaps she'd taken of her friends on Capri, and she'd been quite pleased with some of those at the time.

Oh! The cobalt blue dress she'd had made for that trip must have been what she was wearing the first time she and Eliot had met as adults. It would probably be a mistake to be flattered by his remembering that; the shade, like spending time with her, was simply something he associated with work. Still, she knew she looked good in it and he had said it was delightful…

"These aren't bad at all," Eliot said.

"Don't overdo the praise, will you?"

"Not a chance! However, I will admit you've improved a lot since the start of the trip… and so has your photography."

"Thanks. My stamina is no better though; I'm exhausted."

"Go on then, get yourself into bed. I'll sort out the plates and stuff; I can see you're tired."

She was really glad she hadn't snapped at him. Every time he stopped to help or teach her anything it took him away from his own work. "Thanks, Eliot."

"No problem. Oh, Jess?" he said as she opened the bathroom door.

"Yes?"

"Did you enjoy your mash?"

She'd been so tired and then so distracted by what he was saying she'd eaten it all without even noticing. She dashed into the bathroom and grasped the sink. The expected wave of nausea didn't come. Jess was too tired to try to figure out why not. Perhaps it was something to do with Eliot being nice.

"What is it today?" Jess asked as she served a breakfast of portobello mushrooms topped with crispy bacon and fried cherry tomatoes. "I can't remember if you said St David's Head or if that's after the barbecue."

"It was going to be afterwards, but if you want to see those cute little waddling puffins then we're climbing up there today as well as doing a couple of other shoots."

"Another busy day it is then." Jess ate and cleared up as quickly as she could. Meanwhile Eliot put everything they'd need into their backpacks. He climbed into the driver's seat just as she was putting the last of the crockery away.

"Everything secure?" he asked.

Jess quickly checked the drawers and skylights were all properly closed. "Yep, ready to go."

He waited until she'd fastened her seat belt before

starting the engine. Things between them had definitely improved since the days when he'd punished her, just for being there, by driving off whilst she was still in the back of the van.

The car park for St David's Head was at Whitesands Bay. The moment they turned in, Jess could see both why it had earned its name and that the beach was popular with surfers.

"Have we got time for a few action shots?" she asked.

Eliot opened the door, letting in a blast of shockingly cold air. "You've got ten minutes whilst I put on something warmer."

Jess, already dressed in jeans and long-sleeved top, grabbed her camera and ran down to the water's edge. Almost immediately it was obvious that action photography was something else she had yet to learn. She took just a few shots, mostly so Eliot would be able to tell her where she was going wrong. As she worked the waves crashed and pounded onto the sandy beach in the small bay. The sound seemed be wrapped around her as though chasing itself round in circles looking for an escape.

At either end of the beach, jagged rocks rose up. It wouldn't be easy climbing over those, especially if she had to do so quickly to catch up with Eliot. She looked back to see him waiting beside the van and ran back.

"Three minutes to spare; I'm impressed."

"We're not going along the beach are we? It doesn't look very safe."

"Don't worry, we're using the well-worn path that's been properly maintained by the National Trust."

"Oh, good." That sounded easier, but wouldn't keep her

so warm. "I'm just going to use up one of those three minutes," she said and got back into the van.

She'd put on a thicker sweater, if she could remember where she'd stowed it. She opened one of the overhead lockers and spotted an old, battered book on photographic techniques. Curious, she flipped it open and saw 'Happy 10th birthday, Eliot. Love Mum and Dad'. Tucked inside were several photos, of people she guessed were his family – and what looked like the flowers she'd put into his hand the day they'd visited the ruin.

The delicate violets and tufted vetch, although pressed flat, were still a pale mauve and vibrant purple respectively. The chunkier pink sea thrift bloom wasn't yet fully dry. There was no doubt about it, instead of throwing away the flowers she'd picked, Eliot had kept them safe and added them to what was surely a book of treasured memories.

Chapter 17

Jess didn't want to read too much into Eliot having kept the flowers and couldn't ask for an explanation without it seeming she'd been snooping. She abandoned her search for a sweater. She wasn't feeling cold now and she'd be warmer still by the time she'd lugged all his gear up to wherever it was they were going.

They were barely out of the car park when Jess saw a signpost saying 'St David's Head 1 mile' and started to walk a bit more briskly. Eliot must have seen her look gratefully at it.

"Don't be fooled like I was the first time, that's just the distance to the start of the St David's Head nature reserve. The actual rocks are quite a bit further on."

"Thanks for that good news."

He grinned. "My pleasure!"

The sandy path was narrow and he was in front, so she couldn't help noticing how snugly his trousers fitted. She could see his muscles move as he rose up before her. The rhythmic movement was almost hypnotic. Immediately Jess resolved that the next time they climbed anywhere, she'd make sure she was ahead of him. She was in good shape and her jeans were very well cut. She was confident he'd be forced to do as she was and try to concentrate on the scenery to avoid feeling uncomfortable.

Luckily the scenery was stunning enough to be worth her looking at it. There were beautiful flowers everywhere. Some such as sea thrift and scabious where very familiar to her as they grew in the courtyard garden at home. Others she'd seen rarely or only in books.

"Eliot, what about photographing these flowers?"

"Looking for an excuse to stop already?" he asked, but with a smile.

"Of course not." Jess was a little out of breath, but as she had a perfectly legitimate excuse for stopping, she wouldn't have admitted as much, even if she'd been completely shattered. As it was, her wish to lie down had more to do with what was going on in her imagination than tired muscles; she really should concentrate on her photography and not the gorgeous photographer she was working with.

"The violets?" he asked.

"Those and all the others. I thought it would be nice to see how many different species there are."

"That's not a bad idea. Biodiversity is a big issue for conservation. Most literature seems to concentrate on birds or other wildlife, but plants are a lot easier to spot and much more accessible."

Jess selected the correct lens and started work. Without moving more than a single pace away from where she'd set down her backpack, she photographed nine different kinds of flowers. Eliot didn't have his macro lens with him, so it was up to her to record the variety of flowers.

Eliot did offer advice, but never tried to take the camera away from her and do the job himself. He'd know he could take more shots another time if she messed up, but she liked to think he now trusted her not to do that.

"Frame the smaller ones quite loosely can you? We might want to make the pictures all the same size and I'd like to keep them in the correct ratio to each other."

"OK. Should I try to get the background much the same for all of them?"

"No, a bit of variety would be good, but keep it as bokeh."

"I have no idea what that is."

"Decrease the depth of field so the grass or whatever is out of focus. That'll bring the subject forward and make it more compelling."

"I don't actually know how to do that," she admitted. She'd seen the technique used in his exhibition and admired the effect without knowing the term for it, but hadn't been able to reliably reproduce it herself.

"You just use a wider aperture."

That sounded perfectly straightforward, which meant she'd seem really incompetent if she messed it up. "OK, talk me through that." She lay onto the soft, warm grass and propped herself up on her elbows so she could hold the camera still. Eliot lay on his side next to her.

Having him so close made her clumsy and she fumbled with the controls. Eliot reached out and held the camera for her. The scent of crushed grass mixed with Eliot's masculine smell to create a heady aroma which made her take huge, deep breaths. At least, that's the reason she gave herself for her heavy breathing.

"Select the aperture size. I'd go for f4. Unless you can go lower."

He reached his other arm across her shoulders to point out the appropriate switch.

If she'd rolled onto her side she'd have been in his arms, the camera abandoned as she snaked her arms around his back and pulled him against her. The crashing of the sea was drowned out by the sound of her own blood rushing around her body.

Jess moved her head a little so she could see his face. His expression was intense although she couldn't tell what he was thinking about. Probably the job they were doing. She should think about that too. Reluctantly she dragged her gaze away and flicked round the dial to 2.8. "Is that far enough?"

"Maybe too far."

She switched back to 3.5 and was surprised to hear him chuckle.

"Is that wrong?" she asked.

"Carry on, don't mind me."

She crawled around, photographing as many flowers as she could find.

Eliot kept close, but didn't touch her again. He watched her as she wriggled around into different positions in order to lie close to the plant she wanted to photograph, without having a rock under her hip or brambles tangling her hair.

The flowers, with flat heads, such as yarrow and scabious looked best from above. The delicate white campion had an inflated pouch behind the flower and so she wanted an image of it side on. Buttercups were at their most beautiful with the sun full on them, to reveal the shiny surface of the petals. Sea thrifts, treated in the same manner would have appeared washed out and bland. They were much better backlit, so the pale pink blossoms almost glowed against the clear blue sky, giving an impression of illuminated clouds at sunset. Snowy Queen Anne's lace appeared both dramatic and delicate with a backdrop of dark rock. The stony landscape also served to highlight the intricate shapes of wild orchids.

Eliot seemed amused, rather than annoyed, by the

delay. "As you're so keen on flowers, I'm going to make you do the keywording when we can get online and look up all the names."

Jess nodded. She would need to check she was right about a few of the less common ones and there were a couple of varieties which she didn't know at all, but she'd have wanted to learn their names even if Eliot hadn't needed the information.

A tiny blue butterfly landed on a brilliant yellow trefoil. The combination of colours was exquisite. "Oh look, how pretty is that?" Jess exclaimed.

Eliot squatted in front of her. "Absolutely beautiful."

She glanced up at him and straight into his eyes. For one crazy moment she thought he meant her. That would explain why he'd taken so many photos of her... but of course he was talking about the vibrant contrast of flower and insect.

He looked away from her and down at the butterfly. "I think that's a chalkhill blue," he said as Jess took several shots.

"OK, I think that's everything here."

"You said that like a pro!" Eliot said.

"I can talk the talk at least."

"You can walk the walk too, my girl. Come on."

St David's Head was nowhere near as far away as she'd feared after his warning, but would have been well worth the climb even if it had been three times the distance. It was a huge, dark outcrop of rock. The shape made it easy to appreciate the fearsome power of natural forces which had created it. She could imagine the great surging flow of larva bubbling up through the earth's crust and the steamy, sulphurous hiss as it hit the sea and cooled into fantastic shapes.

Wales was so incredibly beautiful and in a couple of days they'd be sailing over to Skomer to see the puffins. Eliot would take her just because he knew it would make her happy. He liked her, she was sure he did. How else could you explain the faded flowers pressed inside his book?

Jess took off her backpack, put down the tripod and scrambled onto an enormous boulder. She ran, jumping from one hard chunk of solid stone to another with the ease and excitement of a child on her first bouncy castle. She knew she was up high, that the gaps were wide and the rocks hard, but her exhilaration outweighed all fear. She went higher and higher, springing from one to another, eager to reach the top and look down to the sea.

When she reached the summit she laughed with pleasure and turned to look back at Eliot. He too was laughing as he climbed, in a much more sensible manner, below her. He had to go more slowly, burdened as he was with both sets of camera equipment.

"I'm sorry," she called and turned to climb back to him and reclaim her equipment. "I got a bit carried away."

"I noticed." He smiled. "Anyone watching would probably be wondering if mountain goats are native to this area."

"You mean because I'm so incredibly nimble?"

"I was certainly hoping you were. I didn't fancy having to carry you back down again."

Jess had acted a little recklessly. She couldn't say why, but it felt as though she was supposed to run free across the rocks. Maybe she'd imagined St David would keep her safe.

They took scenic photographs until Eliot declared he

was going to get his revenge on her for scaring him with her mountain goat act. He chose two large, smooth surfaced rocks which were surrounded by springy grass, and asked her to repeatedly leap from one to another while he took photos from every possible angle, even lying in the crevice between them to capture her flying through the air above him. That provided plenty of opportunity for him to appreciate how good she looked in her jeans, but he explained the reason was to show how exhilarating it could be to get out and enjoy the countryside.

When he'd finished she flopped down on a patch of grass in the sunshine. "Gosh I'm hungry, I wish I'd brought a picnic."

Eliot unzipped a pouch on his rucksack and produced a pack of mixed nuts and raisins. He made a sound like a mini fanfare as he presented them to her.

"Excellent, thanks."

He'd also brought a bar of mint chocolate, two apples and individual cartons of orange juice. They ate, then lay back in the sun for a few minutes. Soon they were wandering all over the area taking more photos.

Afterwards, they visited two nearby sites to photograph conservation work, which thankfully were both on almost flat ground, before returning to the car park at Whitesands Bay. Eliot declared he wanted to take more shots from a rocky outcrop, during golden hour.

"Don't worry, we haven't got to climb right back up to the top of St David's, just to that bit which looked like a tiny island. The tide's lower now, so we should be able to get out."

To Jess's now very tired legs it felt like a long walk, out over a rough path which was wet from the sea. The ground was unstable and her earlier sure-footedness deserted her as she struggled to balance on the slippery surface whilst carrying a tripod and backpack. The moment she turned down a rutted path through the grassland and was climbing again, her muscles protested and tightened, making every step hard work.

It was getting cold too as the sun dipped behind St David's Head. The warm colours of the sunset only reminded her of the cosy orange sweater she'd still not retrieved from wherever she'd stored it.

"I'm going to shoot the waves crashing onto the rocks below, using a slow shutter speed," Eliot said. He tried to tell her why he thought that was a good idea, but she was too cold and tired to take much interest.

Realising she was in danger of getting grouchy, Jess forced herself to make an effort. She smiled, stepped out briskly and trapped her toes in a small crevice. Unfortunately although they stopped abruptly, the rest of her leg kept going. She yelped.

Eliot glanced back.

"I'm OK," she called. "Shall I wait here? Doesn't look like there's much room and I don't want to get in your way." Plus her ankle felt really uncomfortable and she'd rather not put any weight on it just yet.

"Won't be long," Eliot said.

Maybe he wasn't, but it felt like an hour. When he returned she limped beside him.

"You're really hurt?"

"I don't think it's broken or anything."

"Oh, Jess," he sounded upset. "I thought you'd just stood in a puddle. Come on, lean on me."

He helped her back to the van and left her slumped on a seat as he put their equipment away. When they got to their overnight stop he said, "Why don't you have a hot shower to warm you up a bit and I'll make us a drink."

"I'd better cook dinner, if I don't do it now I don't think I'll be able to do it at all."

"I spotted a chippy just up the road. How about we get a take-away tonight?"

No doubt about it, she was falling in love with him. "Wonderful idea. Will you put the hot water on for me, please."

"It's been heating whilst we drove. Go on, get in the shower. Use as much water as you like, we'll fill up again tomorrow."

As soon as warm water flooded over her Jess started to feel better. It was wonderful to think that all she had to do was get herself warm and dry and then eat hot filling food before crawling into bed next to him.

As she emerged from the bathroom wrapped in towels, Eliot handed her some dry clothes. They consisted of lacy underwear, long socks and her tracksuit. When she came out again wearing everything except the socks, she sank onto the bench seat.

Eliot gave her a mug. "Hot chocolate, with rum."

She smiled gratefully as she sipped the drink. "Oooh, that's good."

"How's the ankle?" Eliot knelt in front of her and examined her feet.

"Not too bad now," she admitted. "I don't think there's any permanent damage."

"Glad to hear it." He massaged both feet gently, then slid his hands higher to rub her aching calves. She put her drink down, concerned that she'd accidentally slop it over him. All the tension had seeped out of her and she just sat back and enjoyed the feeling. His hands moved higher still, but she had to stop him before she embarrassed herself by making it perfectly clear how much she was enjoying the sensation of his warm hands rubbing her bare flesh.

"Are fish and chips OK?" he asked as he put on her socks. "They're not exactly colourful, but I haven't seen any other take-aways around here."

Neither had Jess. If she'd spotted a pizzeria or Chinese restaurant close to anywhere they'd camped she'd have insisted on buying a meal from there instead of cooking when she was so tired.

"It'll be fine. They're not exactly white either and not something Mum ate." That was true, but Lizzie once served her fish with a crispy crumb coating and Jess had felt that awful choking feeling as she'd pushed it around her plate. Of course the fact she'd already been uncomfortable with the idea of Lizzie cooking in Mum's kitchen hadn't helped. Her eating problem had started to get worse after Daddy's engagement but was definitely improving now.

By the time she'd eaten her fish, drunk another hot chocolate laced with rum and curled up in bed next to Eliot she was so warm and comfortable she was almost purring like a cat.

"Eliot, I'm so happy," she murmured before drifting off to sleep.

Jess awoke to hear rain pitter-pattering onto the roof of the campervan. The sound would have been pleasant, had it not reminded her that they had a lot to get done in a short time, and needed good weather in order to keep up with Eliot's hectic schedule. She checked the time and realised golden hour had come and gone; although the light would probably have been more like unpolished pewter than a warm glow. Surely not even Eliot would have her trudging up a mountain in the rain, if only because the water would be bad for his equipment.

No, she wasn't being fair. When she pulled her weight Eliot was perfectly reasonable and pleasant, even seemed to like her. It was only when she was grumpy through tiredness, or complaining about things he'd said she wouldn't like that she felt he regretted having her with him. If she wanted Eliot, and she did, then she'd have to live up to her declaration that she could cope with the workload and living conditions. In the meantime, he was still asleep and she was in bed next to him. She wriggled close and stretched out a hand to touch him. She felt his trim waist, then gradually slid her hand lower, to caress his hip.

"Jess," Eliot murmured in his sleep. He turned right over so he was on his front with an arm around her. She didn't dare move in case she woke him and he moved away. Sleep was impossible as she wondered why he'd called her name in his sleep. Was he dreaming about her? If so what thoughts were going through his mind? If they were the same as the ones in her own head, then she should probably be out the bed before he woke up. She lay still and waited for him to stir.

It wasn't long before he kissed her shoulder and asked her in a bleary voice what time it was.

"It's gone seven."

"I suppose we'd better get up soon then."

"I suppose," she agreed reluctantly.

He turned to face her. "No rush though."

She really should get out of bed. By staying where she

was, Jess was admitting she liked being in bed with him.

"You still happy?" he asked. "Last night you said you were."

"Yes, I am."

"Why?" he brushed loose tendrils of hair from her face.

"I'm warm, dry and not hungry." That was part of it. Maybe in future she wouldn't take such things for granted to the degree she had so far in her life.

"And?"

And Eliot was close to her, interested in her, touching her. She was probably reading far too much into it.

"And I think I'd better get up."

He put his arm around her. "There's a release fee."

"Which is?"

"A kiss."

Chapter 18

What could Jess do? She wanted to agree to his terms. Would that be worse than staying in his arms in bed? She didn't have to decide, because Eliot seemed to take her silence for acceptance and kissed her. His lips barely brushed against hers, but she could feel the effects throughout her whole body. She sighed as he kissed her for a second time. He gazed into her eyes, then kissed the tip of her nose, before releasing her.

"Go make my breakfast, woman," he said.

Jess remembered to collect clothing from the overhead lockers before climbing out of bed. She was careful to put her uninjured foot down first. Thankfully although bruised, the other one didn't produce the expected stab of pain as she tentatively put weight on it.

Jess regretted using so much hot water the night before. Actually, no, she didn't, she regretted not having the strength to help refill the tank. She could have done with a long, cool shower to calm her down before she faced Eliot again. As it was she had to make do with a birdbath. She cleaned her teeth, brushed her hair until it shone and applied plenty of moisturiser. It seemed likely that due to the rain, they'd be in the van more than usual that day, and the bathroom mirror was steam free, so she applied mascara and gave herself a squirt of perfume. She grinned at her reflection as it occurred to her that doing so little already felt like she was fussing over her appearance.

"Do you have any plans for today?" she asked when she emerged, fully dressed, from the bathroom.

"Yes, but I think you're too much of a good girl to go along with them." He was using that wicked grin again. The one which made her wish she was a good girl in the same way that Christina was.

Jess had to keep control of the situation or she was likely to do something she might regret. "I meant with regard to photography," she said in a mock serious tone.

"See what I mean?" he said as he swung his legs over the side of the bed and then dropped down so he was standing upright. "You wanted a lesson in processing. I think this morning would be a good day for that." He took a couple of steps so he was right next to her and put a hand on each of her shoulders. "We can press a few buttons and see what develops."

"Breakfast first though?" She stepped away and pulled open the fridge door, creating a barrier between them.

She'd worked out Eliot was fond of a full English breakfast and happy to give him what he wanted when it came to food. She couldn't help wondering if he was just teasing, or if there really was anything else he wanted from her today. If there were, she might be tempted to give him that too.

Knowing he was most likely just trying to get her flustered didn't help, particularly as it was working. She cooked up a proper fried breakfast for them both. That was partly because it kept her busy and she had to concentrate to get everything cooked and still warm at the same time.

"That was wonderful, Jess, thanks," he said once he'd finished his sausage, bacon, eggs, sautéed potatoes, mushrooms, tomatoes, beans and fried bread. He bent to kiss her cheek as he passed by her to put his plate in the sink and fetch the orange juice she'd forgotten to put out.

"Sorry, there wasn't room for that on the table," she said. She was still eating.

"I knew you'd have a good excuse."

The low water alarm beeped as Jess filled the sink to wash up.

"Blast, I forgot about that last night," Eliot exclaimed.

"Do you have a good excuse?" she asked.

"Mmm hmm, but I'm not sure you'll want to know what was on my mind when I should have been thinking about cold water."

Was what he'd been thinking of when he'd massaged her feet last night, and then suggested they buy supper and have an early night, the same thing she'd been thinking?

Jess had to get a grip of herself. She wanted Eliot, but not just for the last few nights of their trip. He'd said that she was like her father, ready to manipulate people to get what she wanted. She was beginning to see the truth of that even though she also recognised that she herself was sometimes manipulated to an even greater extent by those around her. If she could find the confidence, she was fairly sure she could persuade Eliot to make love to her. She wasn't at all sure she could keep hold of him in the long term – at least not without showing him she'd changed and was no longer Daddy's spoilt little girl. She didn't know how she'd do that, but she'd find a way.

"So, let's get down to business," Eliot said, without making a move towards his computer equipment.

"Yes, let's. Your laptop or mine?"

He chuckled, but was soon concentrating on selecting suitable images. Once he had, Eliot slid the computer over to Jess and told her what to do. They were sitting close together with Eliot often leaning across her to touch the computer keypad. With a real effort Jess managed to concentrate on what his fingers were doing to the keys rather than imagining how they'd feel if she were to complain of stiff muscles and ask him to give her another massage.

Eliot showed her how to increase the contrast, adjust the colour and brighten a dull image. This had briefly been mentioned in college and she'd attempted to use the techniques herself, but with limited success. Her results had all looked obviously processed and artificial. That didn't happen the way Eliot did it.

"The difference is amazing," she said when she compared unprocessed images with those she'd worked on under his instruction.

"But never quite as good as a photo taken under ideal conditions." He brought up images they'd taken very early one morning.

Although they were still raw files, she instantly saw he was right. "You're pretty much obsessed by golden hour, aren't you?"

"It's all about the light, Jess."

"Basically you're saying that I'm never going to be able to sleep late ever again?" Jess asked.

"Of course you can – in bad weather and at midwinter."

"Or give up on being a photographer?" Jess asked.

"I'm starting to believe that's not going to happen."

After they finished a late lunch, of tender beef strips sizzled with mixed peppers and served in crisp lettuce wraps, the rain had stopped.

"Want to take pictures?" Eliot asked, as Jess filled the sink with water ready to wash up.

The sky was a little brighter, but still completely covered with cloud. "Is this light OK?"

"You tell me." He took the plate she'd just washed and dried it.

"I'd say no, not unless there was no other choice. If I could, I'd wait for the sun to come out. I think it's going to."

He nodded. "And if there was no choice?" He used the same tone he had when questioning her about her portfolio in her apartment. That time her answers had helped persuade him to bring her to Wales so he could teach her. This was an opportunity to prove he'd been right to agree.

"Then I'd use a higher ISO and wider aperture… and afterwards process as you've just shown me." Jess was confident not only that her answer was correct, but that she'd really be able to make a reasonable job of all that.

"Nine out of ten. A higher ISO can create a noisy picture and when a lens is used wide open, the image can be soft at the edges."

"Noisy? Is that when it looks kind of grainy?" She'd noticed that in some of her own photos taken in poor light, and that occasionally pictures were less clear towards the edges, but hadn't really understood why.

"That's it."

"I get that's not ideal, but the only alternative would be a much slower shutter speed and if it's too slow the image will be blurry." Again she knew she was right.

"Why?"

"It's not possible to hold the camera perfectly still for

long."

"You could use a tripod."

"I could if you showed me how."

"I suppose I'd better. A tripod is pretty well essential in low light conditions, but it's also valuable if you're using a long exposure to create a special effect," he explained as he demonstrated setting it up and attaching a camera.

"Like car light trails?" She remembered him doing that on their first day. Hard to believe that was little more than a week ago.

"Or to blur water, for night photography, HDR and time lapse."

"I'm beginning to see why you've had me carrying one about most of the time; you never know when it might be useful."

"That, plus with your hands full you can't chuck water over me."

"Want to bet?" She lifted the half-filled washing up bowl in as menacing a manner as possible.

"What I meant was you're far too nice a person to do such a thing, unless it was a total accident."

"Rats, you're right." Jess lowered the bowl and tipped the used water down the sink.

They spent the rest of the day refilling the water tank and then shooting pictures using the tripod. As the sun began to break through they moved into the shade of a tree and then Jess attempted to 'freeze' the water in a stream. They returned to the van, in glorious sunshine, shortly after five. "Perfect timing too, we've got a party to get to," Eliot said.

"I'd better get changed."

"Not yet, I want to try driving out of this field first. It

rained in the night and the van doesn't have the best grip on wet ground."

"You mean we might have to walk?" It had to be at least six miles.

"No, I mean you might have to push."

Eliot was right. Although he'd taken the precaution of parking facing slightly downhill, the van slithered forward only a few feet before the wheels span. By pushing together they managed to free it from the ruts he'd just created.

"OK, I'll try driving again with you pushing," Eliot said.

"You're stronger and heavier than me and haven't recently sprained your ankle. I'll drive."

"Good plan," Eliot said.

But of course he didn't know about the time she'd got Daddy's car stuck in a muddy field belonging to Alyssa's parents, while showing off to her friends. Jess had learned from that mistake though. She could do this. Definitely. Absolutely.

She balanced the clutch, then simultaneously released the handbrake and pressed down hard on the accelerator. The van moved forward straight away. It slithered a little, but was soon safely on the harder ground by the gate.

Jess hadn't been sure if they'd be taking photos at the barbecue, so her camera was still in the accommodation area of the van. She grabbed it intending to take a photo of the rutted ground and the van safely in the distance. Zoe, Alyssa and Christina weren't going to believe her without photographic evidence.

She got more than she'd bargained for. Looking at the scene, it was easy to deduce that Eliot had leant his whole weight against the van, expecting to push hard. When she'd simply pulled away, he'd been sent sprawling and landed in the perfect position to get sprayed in the wet mud kicked up by the wheels. The ground was soft, there was no way she could have hit him and he was on his feet, so she knew he was OK, but with that bewildered expression and a neat, diagonal squirt of mud from his left ear to right kneecap he did look funny. Finally; revenge for making her check she'd removed her lens cap after their riverside picnic. Jess managed to snap a couple of photos before dissolving into giggles.

She almost had herself under control when he reached her and said, "Thanks for the sympathy." That set her off again.

"You can have the bathroom first," she offered. She wasn't being generous; she wanted to download the pictures onto her computer before he could think of deleting them.

Eliot showered and came out wrapped in a towel. "There wasn't much hot water and I've probably used it all," he said. "Serves you right."

Jess was ahead of him. Knowing the water heater hadn't been on long, as they'd not expected to need another shower, she'd boiled a kettle.

"That's cheating," he said as she poured the hot water into the bathroom sink.

"Missed a bit," she said, pointing to his perfectly clean, left ear. She laughed again as he raised his hand to check.

Eliot shook his head as though in disbelief, but whether that was at her silly joke or the fact he'd fallen for it she wasn't sure. It didn't matter though as he was failing to suppress his grin.

Jess washed and changed as quickly as she could. The bathroom mirror steamed up, so she opened the roof vent.

She heard Eliot's laugh; a deep and decidedly attractive sound. Even though it was unlikely to be anything to do with her, Jess was pleased he was happy. She'd do what she could to keep him that way.

She brushed her hair vigorously and so heard nothing more from Eliot until she put on lipstick.

"Poor kid was so exhausted she didn't know what she was doing," he said.

Clearly he was on the phone and he seemed to be talking about her – but who to? And why? He hadn't been laughing when he said that, in fact he sounded sorry for all he'd put her through. That's if it really was her he'd meant.

Jess thought about the people she'd discussed Eliot with. Zoe and Alyssa to moan when she'd thought he was being unfair or unkind. All three of her friends to say how much she liked him, how frustrating it was to sleep next to him, but not with him. Christina, who'd given unsolicited advice on how to change that last one.

Jess had been too exhausted to know what she was doing for most of the last week and Eliot hadn't come into contact with anyone else he'd have reason to regret overworking in that time. Surely he had meant her? It had to mean something that he'd talk to a friend about her. She was going to have to do something to convince him she was no kid, and the beach barbecue might well provide an opportunity.

Chapter 19

Jess added gloss to her lipstick, mascara to her lashes and scent to some of the places she hoped Eliot might get close too and… She really must stop thinking like Christina or she was likely to do something which would either make them very late for the party or be far more embarrassing than sprawling in the mud, depending on whether or not it was reciprocated. Jess ran cold water over her hands and took calming breaths until ready to behave in a way appropriate for an event with Girl Guides in attendance.

When she stepped out of the bathroom she saw Eliot in the driver's seat ready to go. She thought, or maybe just hoped, she saw approval in his expression as he watched her settle herself in the cab and fasten her seat belt.

The Major greeted them at the lane to his house, explaining he'd set out traffic cones and a 'reserved' sign, to ensure there was sufficient room for Eliot to park the campervan.

"The wifi works where I've put you. Stay as long as you like and give me a shout in the morning if you'd like breakfast or water or anything."

They thanked him and drove off leaving The Major to welcome the queue behind them. There were more signs directing guests to the car parking area, toilet facilities in his home, the bar, barbecue area and to the beach.

"I bet he had fun organising everything," Jess said as

they headed for the bar.

"I imagine he did. Looks like he's done a good job."

When Jess saw the trestle tables covered in white cloths and set out with a huge selection of plastic glasses, ice buckets and drinks she had to agree. She guessed it was also The Major who'd supplied the soft drinks; sparkling mineral water, fruit juice and Coke. Six of each kind were neatly displayed. The wine, beer and other alcoholic drinks were a very varied selection, suggesting everyone who'd already arrived had brought something different. Many of the bottles were no longer quite full. Jess deposited their contributions and Eliot poured them each a glass of wine from one of the bottles she'd brought. They took their drinks, and the open bottle, and walked in the direction everyone else seemed to be headed.

Most guests were on the beach where music was playing and a huge bonfire blazed. They chatted to the volunteers they'd met previously, declined an invitation to join a team for rounders and assured numerous people they really were off duty and wouldn't take any embarrassing photos. Groups grew and shrank, people were urged to dance to such timeless classics as 'The Birdie Song' and *'Y.M.C.A.'*, but Eliot was never away from Jess's side for long. He did leave her to it when Llewellyn came to coax her into dancing to 'The Macarena' with him. Jess spotted him being taught the moves by a group of Girl Guides and hoped that wouldn't mean he'd be reluctant to dance any slower numbers later on.

The Major banged a gong to attract everyone's attention and announced the food was ready. As Jess took a step to follow the surge, Eliot reached for her hand.

"There'll be a queue already," he said. Without letting

go of her hand he walked a short way along the beach and revealed where he'd hidden the wine bottle.

They sipped their drinks, looking out to sea and sitting so close she could feel the warmth from his body. Jess had to keep both hands on her wineglass to stop her reaching out and running her fingers through his sexily tangled hair, or along his jaw towards his lips, or…

"You OK? Jess?" Eliot asked.

She took a deep, steadying breath. "I'm sure The Major has enough food to go round."

Eliot gave that sexily deep chuckle of his again. "You've demoted him! Apparently the locals have nicknamed him The Admiral."

"Do you think he knows?"

"I expect so, but he'd never let on in case he had to deny it. That's not what I meant though."

"I'm fine." She wasn't sure exactly what he had meant and it seemed that had showed.

"I've been very hard on you. The long hours, attempts to make you give up, the mash…"

"That was all deliberate?"

"Not with the mash. I'm sorry I got you to make it, but I was tired too and forgot about your… problem until I saw your plate after you'd eaten it. I shouldn't have said anything, but I was pleased because I thought you were getting over it. It's not that simple, is it?"

It wasn't, but Jess was starting to believe that, with time, it really would become much less of an issue. Lizzie had once suggested she talk to someone about her phobia and mentioned someone who'd had excellent results in treating eating disorders. Jess had been horrified that Lizzie had noticed her difficulty and hotly denied any sort of problem. In those days she wouldn't have accepted any kind of help from her father's fiancée, but perhaps when she got home she'd ask Lizzie if she still had the number.

Jess realised she'd been quiet for a few moments and not wanting Eliot to think he'd distressed her, said, "You didn't have me climb that same mountain six times by accident!"

"I'm sure it was only five, but I am sorry. I thought you'd quit and wanted to get that over with, then because I'd wasted time on that and walking miles to places we could have got to in the van, there was catching up to do."

Jess had already worked some of that out. "But you still spent time teaching me."

"You were carrying out your part of the deal, I thought I should do the same."

"So I have been useful some of the time?"

"Yep – and you're a much better cook than me."

"Gosh, that was almost a compliment!"

"Almost. You're clever, resourceful, hard-working and very pretty. And when you're not being a poor little rich kid, you're good company."

That was better, but he was thinking of her as a kid again. She really must put that right. Not now though; there were too many people about and she was really hungry.

Jess's comment that there would be enough food left proved to be correct. She soon had a plateful of succulent roasted pork coated in a sweet rich sauce, spicy chicken wings, crunchy coleslaw and watercress. Eliot ate his hog roast in a chunk of buttered French bread and followed it with a vegetable kebab and sausages.

As she ate, Jess thought of all she'd learned during her

time working with Eliot. Photography seemed only a small part of that. Now she really appreciated being warm, dry, full of good food and wine and not having to climb anywhere. Until this last week she could have had that anytime she wanted, but it just seemed normal. She doubted she'd ever be quite so dismissive of physical comfort again. She'd also know she could cope with a certain amount of discomfort. She'd be prepared to work for what she wanted. Having Eliot in her future was the thing she wanted most. What could she do to make that a reality?

A few people stayed in the barbecue area to eat the last scraps of food, but most returned, via the bar area, to the beach. Music was playing again; Meatloaf's 'I'd Do Anything For Love 'belted out over the sand.

Although still producing plenty of heat, the bonfire had died down considerably.

"Time for the marshmallows," Eliot said.

"No one will want them after the lovely food we've just eaten," Jess said.

"Didn't I tell you to trust me?"

Unsure whether or not he was playing some kind of joke on her, Jess fetched the bags of marshmallows and packs of chocolate biscuits from the van, and gave them to the Guide leader. She certainly looked pleased with the unusual gift.

A few minutes later, the Girl Guides were all toasting marshmallows on sticks over the fire. Once the sweets were caramelised and crispy on the outside, they sandwiched them between biscuits, chocolate sides inwards. It was clearly something they'd done before and were delighted to do again.

When they offered one to Jess and Eliot, he said, "We'll

have a pink one, please." He broke the biscuit sandwich in half, pulling out long strands of gooey marshmallow rather like mozzarella cheese on a pizza.

The combination of cold biscuit, red hot filling and melted chocolate was very sweet with hints of twig and a touch of burned sugar, yet wasn't as disgusting as she'd expected. She'd probably have loved them when she was the same age as these girls.

"Would you like to dance?" Eliot asked, offering exactly what she most wanted at that moment; to be in his arms.

If she'd thought she was happy before, she was in heaven as he held her close and they gently swayed with the music. She closed her eyes and put her head on his shoulder. Jess wanted to stay like that forever. She was sure that anyone glancing in their direction would see a replica of the gorgeous photograph of the sunset, with them both silhouetted against the sky, which Eliot had taken a couple of days previously.

'Save A Prayer' faded into 'Moon River' and 'Nothing Compares 2 You,' as they danced. Eventually Eliot said, "Come on, Jess. It's time for bed."

It couldn't be very late; it wasn't yet completely dark and some of the older Girl Guides were still there. She, at least, had slept in that morning. It seemed quite possible Eliot had something other than sleep on his mind when he took her by the hand and lead her unresistingly away.

Back in the van Jess asked, "Do we have an early start tomorrow?"

"Not particularly, but we do have a busy day."

"Right."

"Something is bothering you." Eliot stepped close and put his hands on the top of her arms.

"I was just wondering why we left the party so early." She could hear that her voice was husky and guessed her eyes were inviting a response which had nothing to do with golden hour or the distance they'd have to travel to the first shoot of the day.

"Because I wanted to do this." He pulled her close and kissed her.

Jess slid her arms around his waist and kissed him back. Her heart was beating fast, first with nerves and then as he responded to her kiss, with passion and longing. Jess heard herself moan with pleasure.

A knock on the side of the van made both Jess and Eliot jump. They stopped kissing and pulled slightly apart.

Chapter 20

Eliot dropped his arms to Jess's waist and called, "Hello?"

"I forgot to give you the wifi code earlier," The Major replied.

"Argh!" Eliot let go of Jess and opened the van door.

The Major put one foot inside the van, but seemed to realise there wasn't room for anyone else. "I saw you heading back here and knew you'd be working."

As it wasn't yet nine, that was a reasonable assumption. Jess switched on her phone in an effort to look busy, as Eliot opened his laptop and typed in the code. She thought he'd been annoyed by the interruption, but as he frowned at the computer screen his expression grew much darker than it had been when The Major had knocked on the van.

Eliot had only kissed her for a very short time, but it was long enough for Jess to forget they were parked on The Major's driveway and not back in their field, away from everyone else. Had Eliot too lost sight of reality? He'd made it so clear that this was to be a working trip and nothing more. If the kiss was because of a momentary physical attraction on his part, which seemed painfully likely, he'd probably resent having given in to it. A brief affair might last the few remaining days of the trip, but after that she'd lose him forever.

"Is it not working?" the Major asked.

"It's fine, thanks." Eliot didn't sound convinced.

"I'll leave you to it then. Will you join me for breakfast?"

Eliot didn't respond, so Jess said, "That's very kind, but we'll probably be away very early, because of the light."

"Ah, right you are."

"Goodnight and thank you so much for a lovely party."

Eliot was still concentrating on his laptop and Jess's phone had been beeping. She checked and saw she'd had several missed calls from her father's landline that afternoon and a more recent text from Lizzie. She opened it and read, *Jess, please give me a call.*

"Daddy? No!" Last time she'd spoken to him, she'd asked him not to interfere in her life and now…

"Actually, it's quite a good move."

"How can this be good?" Jess demanded, waving her phone at him.

"What's wrong?" Eliot read the message. "It's just a text asking you to call."

"But why?" As soon as she said it Jess realised that bad news about her father wasn't the only possible reason for Lizzie to contact her.

"I expect she's emailed you the details."

Jess checked and saw he was right.

Hi Jess,

Sorry if I'm being a nuisance. Your dad said you didn't want to be interrupted during this trip, but I felt sure you'd want to know what was happening.

It seems that a couple of years ago a nuclear power company had expressed an interest in buying some land around Dibden Spit. Nothing came of it, but concerns were raised by the RSPB and the Wildlife and Wetlands Trust, and there were protests from local groups too.

That's partly why the sale didn't go through. When your dad made enquiries, it seems some of those same people assumed he wanted it for development. They've arranged a demonstration on Thursday. That's the tenth anniversary of Beaulieu Nature Reserve, so local press and TV will be in the area and this is likely to get covered too.

Your dad said telling them our intentions were good wouldn't work so well as showing them and suggested I arrange a beach clean for the same day. I think it's a great idea – any protesters who really care about the area or wildlife should join us and we'll have them on side for when we start properly. So that's what I'm doing.

There's no need to cut your trip short. I've got everything sorted out, not that there was much to do, but like I said I thought you'd want to know our project was starting rather earlier than we'd expected.

Love Lizzie.

Jess wasn't sure how to react. She'd expected and wanted to work with Eliot on the clean-up at Dibden Spit, and photograph it from start to finish. She half wanted to be angry at Lizzie for taking over. It had been Daddy's idea though and he was extremely hard to say no to.

Eliot said it wasn't a bad move; he obviously knew all about it now, but like her had only just heard. The Dibden Spit project was so important to him he'd agreed to bring Jess to Wales and because he had, it was now starting without him.

"Sorry, I asked Daddy not to interfere in this trip. It seems as though he over reacted and decided we shouldn't be contacted at all."

"Or guessed I'd want to go down there and cut this trip, and therefore your training, short?"

"Do you?" Jess asked.

"Sadly a one day clean-up won't have much impact, so I'll have plenty more chances to photograph what needs to be done."

That didn't answer her question. He was just trying not to make her feel bad if he missed it on her account. "But you do want to go?"

"I would like to be there from the start. But I promised to take you over to Skomer. If we go to Dibden Spit you'll miss out on seeing the puffins."

She'd really been looking forward to that, but it wouldn't hurt her to not get what she wanted for once. Thursday's work at Dibden Spit might be of limited effect, but every piece of fishing line they picked up could save a bird's life and they'd be helping ensure the overall success of the project.

"You didn't actually promise, just said we'd try. Anyway, I can go to Skomer another time and the longer I leave it the better photographer I'll be."

"Thanks, Jess." He squeezed her hand. "It'll be hard work. We were already trying to make up a day and it's almost a five hour drive down to the New Forest."

"Looks like we'll have another early start tomorrow after all."

"I'll make it up to you. That really is a promise."

They were up at five and in position to take pictures by first light on the morning after the barbecue. The day seemed to go by at a run, but she enjoyed the knowledge she was helping Eliot achieve something which mattered to him and the fact they were working together as a team.

By the time they stopped, in a large and remote lay-by

that evening, she'd have been happy to just warm up a breakfast in a can. As she'd not bought a replacement for the one they'd eaten the week before they had to make do with pan fried Welsh lamb steaks in a rosemary and red wine sauce, accompanied by sautéed potatoes, and watercress and beetroot salad. They drank the wine leftover from the sauce with it and finished the meal with blue cheese on pumpernickel crackers.

"I'm really going to miss your cooking," Eliot said.

"Not to mention my charming personality and wonderful sense of humour."

"No, better not mention those!"

"Just for that, you can wash up."

"Don't I always?"

"No."

He washed the dishes and left her to finish drying and putting everything away as Jess used the bathroom. When she emerged, wearing her pyjamas, he was rubbing his shoulder.

Tired though she was, Jess couldn't resist the chance to touch him. "Want a back massage?"

"That would be great, thanks."

"You'd better lie on the bed."

Jess started by kneeling at his side, but found that awkward. She manoeuvred so she was astride him, her thighs each side of his hips. She leant right forward, her breasts pressed against his back as she kneaded his shoulders. She inched her way down his spine, working each vertebrae, releasing the tension. From the way he groaned as she moved her hands over his back, down his sides and towards his hips he was either in agony or really enjoying what she was doing to him. When her arms were as tired as her legs were from all the walking, she stopped and lay at his side.

Eliot didn't move. "That was wonderful, thank you."

"You're welcome." She was tempted to suggest he repay her in kind, but resisted. She was sure now that he was attracted to her. If his feelings didn't go deeper, then a night's intimacy wouldn't make up for a failure to finish the current job and get down to the New Forest in time for the clean-up, due to lack of sleep.

"I said I'd make it up to you for missing the puffins."

"You did." She wriggled a little closer. They could still take photographs if they had an hour less sleep, couldn't they?

"Apparently there's a really nice spa in the New Forest. Shall I book you in for Thursday?"

"That's sweet of you." She tried not to let her disappointment show. It was a nice thought and perfect for the old Jess. Or maybe not. A couple of weeks ago it wouldn't have seemed that much of a treat. Now, after her experience of campervan living, hard work and little sleep, she'd probably be far more appreciative of a bit of pampering. It would be great too if she was looking her best when he said goodbye to her and not tired from the trip and mud spattered after helping at Dibden Spit.

Jess knew that once he'd taken her home Eliot would have to finish processing the last of his pictures from Wales and get ready for his next job. Did he plan to do that while she was in the spa? Or perhaps, as he was in need of a rest himself, he would join her. That would be really, really nice.

"Sounds like bliss."

"Right, I'll sort that out then." He sighed. "Now let me get some sleep, will you?"

She kissed his shoulder. "I can't think how I might keep you awake."

"I can, but I remember you telling me you're not that sort of girl and actually I'm not that sort of man."

"I know, but things are different now."

"Oh, Jess…" He turned to face her. "I like you a lot."

"I like you too, Eliot."

"I don't want to hurt you."

But he was going to, she could tell.

"We're very different and you're soon going to go back to your life and I'll go back to mine. They aren't compatible."

"In what way?" She didn't even have a lifestyle now she'd left college. She could do whatever she wanted, as long as Eliot was willing to keep her by his side.

"It's difficult to explain without it sounding as though I'm criticising you."

"That hasn't stopped you pointing out my faults before…"

"Jess, there's nothing wrong with you," he interrupted. "You're a lovely girl. A bit spoiled and used to getting your own way but that's not your fault. You'll be happy with the right man. Someone who shares your interests and whose lifestyle is compatible with yours."

"I think I've found him." She tried to convince Eliot he was that man, but a lump in her throat made it difficult to speak.

"Wow!" Jess said as she stepped out of the van on Wednesday morning. "Now I see why we parked here."

Mist hid the valley, and all evidence of human

existence, from view. All Jess could see was dark mountains glistening in the very first of the light as though sprinkled with diamonds, and the sky streaked with molten gold and rubies.

From then on everything went right. The people Eliot had arranged to meet arrived on time and the locations were ready for them. When viewing a scene Jess spotted litter and rushed to clear it before Eliot could ask. She had learned enough to predict which piece of equipment he might ask for next and to have it ready.

At one point Eliot said, "Nurse, scalpel please."

She handed him the lens he needed just as he disconnected the one attached to his camera. After she'd returned the discarded one to his camera bag, she dabbed his forehead with a lens cloth and was rewarded with his deep sexy laugh. That extremely brief game of doctors and nurses was all they had time for.

Lunch was a burger bought from a van at the side of the road and eaten as they drove on to the next job.

"I asked for extra relish on yours, so keep it in the wrapper as you eat it or you'll get covered."

"Why did you do that?" Jess wasn't particularly fond of relish and couldn't think why he'd suppose she was.

Eliot just shrugged.

The answer came after she'd finished eating; it was so he could mention it and make her think of red sauce, not the white bread roll. That was clever; an extension of the way she used strong flavours, colourful sauces and garnishes to help her cope with food she'd otherwise struggle to eat. In future, if troubled by the appearance or blandness of a food item, she'd mentally add colour and interest. Visualising sunrises she'd shared with Eliot would do that.

Their final task was to photograph a newly installed composting toilet, located along a popular walking route.

"It's ingenious," Eliot explained. "No need to lay pipes or use chemicals and you can imagine what people did before this was provided."

As they climbed towards it, Jess was reminded of her climb in Capri and the photograph Eliot had criticised for showing the view but not the path. "If we photographed it right in the distance, it would show how remote it is and help explain why it's needed," she said.

"You're learning, aren't you? I intended to do that, but we need to be a bit closer than this."

Ten minutes later he took a few shots. "I'll do some more on the way back."

Jess nodded. The light was likely to be better then, as long as they were finished before the sun sunk below the hilltop.

"Can you hold the door open?" Eliot asked when they reached their destination. "Otherwise it just looks like a shed."

Jess did as he asked, doing her best to look like a hiker happy to have reached such facilities. "It's the glamour which makes people want to be photographers, isn't it?"

"Of course not," he sounded indignant. "There's the luxurious lifestyle too, and the very generous working hours."

As they walked back, he said, "Despite the superb model, I admit these pictures aren't quite as pretty as this morning's sunrise."

"Maybe not, but there's a sort of beauty about providing a facility which makes using this area more pleasant and helps to preserve it."

He stopped to look at her. Was he starting to realise how alike they were below the surface?

"We've done brilliantly today. That gives us a choice. We can stay around this area, have a nice view to eat our dinner by and a reasonably early night, or we can drive on a bit further and have the luxury of sleeping in until six."

"Either is fine with me."

"Then we'll go on and break up the drive a bit."

As they drove, Jess mentally assessed the contents of the fridge and tried to think of a meal she could create with what remained. When they stopped, at a small campsite, she hastily prepared a Spanish omelette.

"How is it that I always cook an omelette on the last night of a trip and mine looks exactly like the mix of leftovers it is, but when you do the same think it looks and tastes great?" Eliot asked.

"Just like photography, cooking is a skill that you can learn if someone shows you how and you get in a bit of practise."

"There's hope for me yet then?"

"Definitely." And for them. He must realise by now they were compatible and see how much they could help each other. Surely he did?

Chapter 21

The campsite they booked into had plenty of taps to fill water tanks, and they could connect up to mains electricity, which was convenient for heating water and charging their equipment. The ground was level and well drained, there was a small shop and toilet facilities on site. Only a few spaces remained, proving its popularity, but Jess was already missing the empty field which had been their base for most of the trip.

They didn't get to sleep in until six as a crying baby woke them at five. Or maybe it wasn't the baby so much as a man from the next caravan yelling at the parents to shut it up.

After half an hour, Eliot said, "Shall we go? Maybe we can find somewhere quiet for breakfast."

The service station wasn't quiet. It wasn't very clean either and the food was unappetising. They didn't stay long. And didn't get far before they were stuck in traffic.

Eliot switched on the radio. After a few minutes they learned the delay was because a lorry had shed its load, an hour previously and two junctions ahead.

"There's a map in the door bin." Eliot said. "See if we can come off at the next exit and go round."

"OK."

Once she'd found the right page, it didn't take Jess too long to work out that wouldn't be easy. "We'd have to go a long way off course and it looks like quite minor roads."

"Better stick with the motorway then."

She felt she'd let him down. His mood didn't improve when she tried to talk about what they'd be doing at Dibden Spit. Perhaps he was worried they'd arrive late, or perhaps just irritated by her talking when he was listening out for traffic reports.

She kept quiet until they were past the hold up. Then she asked him about his next job.

"Actually it's a wedding. Not something I'd normally do, but I rashly donated a photo shoot from me as a prize in a charity raffle."

"You could have said it was just for one person," Jess pointed out.

"I was trying to, but the winner was so excited that I couldn't get a word in."

Jess wasn't so sure about that; more likely he hadn't wanted to disappoint them. "And after that?"

"I'll have to get as much as possible done towards the exhibition your father is sponsoring before flying out to La Palma in the Canaries."

She didn't want to discuss the exhibition and the role she might play in it while he was frustrated with the delay in the traffic, so asked, "Have you been there before?"

"A couple of times, but I'm looking forward to going back. I'm not knocking our own scenery, but the Caldera is spectacular. Can you imagine driving up from sea level, past the banana plantations and through the clouds, to the edge of a volcano and looking down into it?"

"Not really, but I'd love to see it."

He ignored her hint. "And lower down there's a subtropical forest. Some of the plant species there aren't found anywhere else on earth. Because of its importance it's been given UNESCO status."

"Is that what you'll be photographing?"

"I'll visit, but just as a tourist for that part. My job is to record the work being done to preserve native plant species around the observatories on La Palma." He explained the measures in place to protect them from humans and wild animals, until sustainable populations once again covered the volcanic peaks of El Roque de Los Muchachos. "Because it's an island the plants have developed independently of those in other areas."

"Like on the Galapagos?"

"Sort of. There aren't quite such startling differences, but some of the plants are unique to the island and distinct even from those on other Canary Islands. There's a form of echium which is pink on Tenerife, but blue on La Palma."

"That's interesting. I grow echium vulgare at home and that has flowers which change from blue to pink as they age. I wonder if it's a variation of the same species."

"I'd have to look up the Latin, but this one takes six years to flower and then reaches three metres in height."

"Definitely not the same! I'd love to see that." This time the remark was spontaneous, rather than intended as a hint, yet received a better response.

"You'd be in your element photographing those and the Canary bellflower, wild freesias and heather trees. They're further apart and harder to get to than those at St David's Head, but I'm sure you'd consider them worth the effort."

As he spoke, Jess could easily imagine the colours and scents of the flowers, the rocky terrain, and Eliot offering advice as she captured it all with her camera. There was nothing to stop her doing just that, assuming Eliot wanted her along. She'd persuaded him to take her to Wales, when he'd not liked her much and hadn't believed she'd be of any help. Things were now very different. Once they'd cleared litter from the area at Dibden Spit which was so important to him, and she'd had an hour or so in the spa to get properly clean and fragrant, he wasn't going to be able to resist.

When they reached the edge of the New Forest, Jess thanked him for all he'd done to help her.

"Just sticking to the deal we made."

"It's much more than that. I know my photography has improved massively, but… well, I have too haven't I?"

"Not massively, no. You weren't horrible before, just a bit…"

"…spoiled and used to getting my own way, I know."

"And I was too used to living and working alone and really grouchy. Sorry about that."

"You're forgiven. And now you can see the advantages of sharing your life with someone, especially if she can cook and knows one end of a camera from the other."

"Well, I…"

"And I've got over that silly thing about not eating white foods."

"Be careful there, Jess. You do seem to be coping much better, but it's only been a few days. If you've struggled with this for years, you can't expect an instant cure. Lizzie says…"

"Lizzie? What's she got to do with…?" Instantly Jess recalled the telephone conversations he hadn't wanted her to hear and the way he'd seemed to know more about her past than she'd told him. "It was her! You've been talking to her about me, haven't you?"

"Of course I have. I was worried, after you ate that mash, that I'd pushed you into it and might have added to your problem. She's my friend, she cares about you and she has some experience of eating disorders. A lot of models do."

He spoke so reasonably that Jess forced herself to calm down before replying. What he'd said made sense. Lizzie knew them both so was the obvious person for him to confide in.

Jess remembered Lizzie's offer to put her in touch with someone who helped those with eating disorders and recognised that had been another kindness Jess had rebuffed. No doubt some of her colleagues, maybe even Lizzie herself, would have struggled to maintain both a model's figure and a healthy relationship with food. That would explain why she'd noticed Jess's problem, even though Daddy hadn't.

"She's been nice about that," Jess admitted.

"She's a nice person. That's why I believed her when she said you were too, deep down, and agreed to take you to Wales."

"Oh."

"She was right. You're lovely, Jess. I just wish… Anyway, have a nice time. The booking is in your name and it's all paid for. I'll pick you up about five-thirty."

They'd stopped outside a gorgeous redbrick mansion. In front was a large sign, welcoming visitors to the New Forest Hydrotherapy Spa Complex.

"I'm going to stay here all afternoon?"

"Six hours of pure bliss to help you recover from all I've put you through and make up for missing the puffins."

Pure bliss was the phrase she'd used, when she thought

she might be sharing the experience with him. He'd taken the trouble to arrange this for her, thinking it was what she wanted. It would be throwing his kind gesture in his face to tell him he'd got it wrong.

"Thanks, Eliot." She grabbed her jacket, kissed his cheek and climbed out.

She watched him drive away, before trudging across the weed-free, raked gravel and then up wide stone steps.

Chapter 22

The door swung open automatically as Jess approached, revealing a flower-filled and very grand hallway.

The beautifully made-up receptionist beamed at Jess. "Welcome. You must be Miss Borlase."

"Yes." How had she worked that out?

"We were told you'd probably like a shower as soon as you arrived. Would you like to do that before you discuss treatment options?"

"I suppose so." Ah, she was the only client who looked to be in need of a wash.

"I'll get someone to arrange that and bring you a robe. Please take a seat for a moment."

Jess sank into a soft sofa, accepted a glass of ice cold green tea, and tried to enjoy the experience as much as Eliot assumed she would. In just a few moments she'd be deluged with unlimited hot water. She could stay in the shower, without low water alarms or grumpy photographers complaining, until perfectly clean and thoroughly rinsed. Even then she needn't get out until she was ready to wrap a fluffy robe around her tired body and decide what should happen to her next.

A 'treatment menu' informed her that hot pebbles, seaweed wraps, volcanic mud packs and beach sand scrubs were all on offer. Jess could soak in herbal infusions, swim through mineral enriched seawater or be spritzed with the energising water obtained from mountain springs. Maybe she'd have a massage to soothe her aching legs. Or a facial to make up for having abandoned her usual beauty regime for almost a fortnight. A manicure? Pedicure? Have her frizzy hair tamed? No doubt the beautician would, the moment she saw Jess, agree they were all needed. There was time for them all too. Lots and lots of time and relaxing, beautiful surroundings in which to waste it.

The warm air was full of the scent of exotic aromatherapy oils. Towards the end of the trip, there had been a slight hint of used socks in the campervan whenever they returned after it had been shut up for a while. The smell hadn't been awful, and quickly dispersed once a window was opened, but ylang-ylang and frangipani were definitely an improvement. Jess inhaled deeply.

Pleasant, gentle music tinkled in the background. The walls and furnishings were in soothing blues and greens. This colour range was picked up in the pretty framed seascapes and even the posters advertising different treatments. Everything about the spa was perfect until she caught sight of her own reflection in a sparkling mirror.

Jess didn't fit into these surroundings. Her hair was a bit wild and clothes far from elegant, but it wasn't just her appearance which was wrong. If she, Alyssa, Zoe and Christina had encountered problems on their journey to Capri and arrived looking dishevelled then they'd just have appreciated the holiday even more. Jess could imagine spending a day here with them all and having fun. She could also imagine, far more clearly, enjoying being here with Eliot.

Naturally being alone wasn't as appealing as being with friends or the man she loved, but it wasn't only that. A long hot shower was a luxury she'd been dreaming of.

Why then wasn't it as enticing as collecting litter on a marshy, possibly polluted, beach and taking photos of others doing the same thing?

Perhaps because she could have a proper shower when she got home that evening. She could book herself into a salon and have her skin moisturised, nails painted and hair blow-dried tomorrow. Right now she could make much better use of her time. Maybe Eliot's doubts she felt that way were the reason he considered them incompatible?

Jess approached the receptionist. "I'm sorry, but something has come up. Could you give me the number of a taxi firm?"

The girl quickly provided a card and asked if there was anything else she could do to help.

"No, thanks."

Nobody could help her with what she must do next. She had to prove to Eliot that she belonged by his side, working towards things they both thought important, rather than wasting time in luxurious surroundings.

When the taxi driver arrived Jess asked him to take her to Dibden Spit.

"Whereabouts, love?"

"I'm not sure. There's a beach clean organised for today."

"Guess that'll be down the end then. You joining in are you?"

"That's right."

"No offence, but you don't seem the type. More like someone who'd be booked in there." He waved a hand back towards the spa.

Jess warmed to the man. He at least didn't think she looked in desperate need of a shower and intensive grooming. "You're not the only person to think that. My... friend thought so too and booked me in for the day."

"You want my opinion, you're nuts to want to go collecting litter in smelly mud, rather than having a nice spa treatment. Not that you need it, mind."

"Exactly. Either way I'll get covered in mud and seaweed, so I might as well do some good."

"One way of looking at it, I suppose." He didn't sound convinced, but kept any further opinions to himself.

Jess gazed out of the window, trying to ignore the litter and concentrate on the beauty of the flat, heather and gorse covered moorland. She saw a deer by the side of the road, surrounded by people who seemed to be taunting it. "Stop!"

The driver braked sharply. "What is it? Oh, poor thing's tangled up."

"Come on, looks like they need help." Jess ran to join those who were trying to coax the deer into a corner so they could catch it and then free it from the plastic netting around its head and front legs.

"Once it's cornered everyone needs to move in close and push it against the fence," a man instructed. "Keep it as still as you can."

The group moved slowly, herding it to a position from which it couldn't easily escape.

"Now!"

Jess launched herself towards the deer. She helped with holding the animal still as those towards the front cut away the netting.

"OK, release."

Before Jess could step away, she was flying backwards into the mud.

The taxi driver helped her up. "Are you OK, love? You look very pale."

Jess didn't see the deer leap away. She could see two identical taxi drivers though and feel herself falling.

Someone caught her. They lowered her onto the ground and put something soft under her head. Her hair was gently brushed away from her face. "Just lie still, sweetheart."

"Eliot? What are you doing here?"

"I could ask you the same thing. I left you somewhere comfortable and safe."

"Because you thought we're different and I'd prefer that to working?"

"Because that's what I feared. Then as I drove off I realised you'd misunderstood about the spa and hadn't meant you wanted to do that instead of helping out on the beach. I wondered if I'd got it wrong and we're not so different after all."

"We're not."

"Maybe, but it doesn't matter. You were right, I do want someone in my life, someone who can cook and knows one end of a lens from the other. Not just anyone. I want it to be you, Jess. I love you."

"And I love you too."

Eliot knelt beside her, pulled her up into his arms and kissed her.

"Leave her be. Poor lass was kicked in the head," the taxi driver said.

"Jess, were you?"

"I think I might have been."

"Saw it myself," the taxi driver said. "Luckily one of the people who stopped to help with the deer is a doctor. She's just fetching her bag."

The doctor examined Jess, asked her and the taxi driver a few questions and then said she appeared to be fine. "Take things easy today though and if you experience any headaches or dizziness get yourself taken into A & E."

"I'll look after her," Eliot assured the doctor.

Eliot paid the taxi driver and then walked Jess back to the campervan. She could have managed perfectly well without his arm around her, but she didn't object.

"What do you want to do now?" Eliot asked as they walked. "It might be best to take you back to the spa."

"Looking like this? I doubt they'd let me in. Take me to Dibden Spit and put me to work."

"The doctor said you should rest."

"No, she said to take things easy. Picking rubbish off flat ground will be easier than hauling tripods up mountains. And you said you'd look after me and you can't if we're in different places."

"I'll come with you. I wouldn't mind a hot shower and a massage myself."

"That can be arranged, but not yet. I'd feel terrible if you didn't get to Dibden Spit because of me."

"I think I've said this before, but you can be very persuasive." He kissed her again.

Jess was sure the way her legs decided they could no longer hold her up and she had to cling to him for support was only temporary and nothing to do with the deer accidentally kicking her.

Eventually Eliot released her and opened the van door. "Are you absolutely sure?"

"I am, but you'll still owe me for missing out on the puffins."

"That's true. How can I make it up to you?"

"A trip to La Palma to photograph wild flowers would do it."

"The air is thinner up on those mountains. You might struggle to carry all your gear."

"I might, but I won't quit."

"I believe you."

The next thing she wanted to persuade him was that her place tonight were the ideal time and location for a hot shower and steamy massage. That probably wasn't going to be too difficult.

I hope you enjoyed this book. If you did, I'd really appreciate a short review on Amazon, Goodreads or anywhere else.

To learn more about my writing life, hear about new releases and get a free short ebook, news and competitions, sign up to my newsletter – subscribepage.io/ItLSNa or you can find the link on my website patsycollins.co.uk

More books by Patsy Collins

Novels

Firestarter
Escape To The Country
A Year And A Day
Paint Me A Picture
Acting Like A Killer

Little Mallow cosy mystery series

Disguised Murder and Community Spirit in Little
Mallow
Dependable Friends and Deceitful Neighbours
in Little Mallow
Deadly Words and Innocent Gossip in Little Mallow

Short story collections

Over The Garden Fence
Up The Garden Path
Through The Garden Gate
In The Garden Air
Beyond The Garden Wall

No Family Secrets
Can't Choose Your Family
Keep It In The Family
Family Feeling
Happy Families

All That Love Stuff
With Love And Kisses
Lots Of Love
Love Is The Answer

Slightly Spooky Stories I
Slightly Spooky Stories II
Slightly Spooky Stories III
Slightly Spooky Stories IV
Slightly Spooky Stories V

Just A Job
Perfect Timing
Coffee & Cake
A Way With Words
Criminal Intent
Crime In Mind
Days To Remember
Making A Move
A Clean Bill Of Health
Your Good Health

Non-fiction

From Story Idea To Reader: an accessible guide
to writing fiction
(co-written with Rosemary J. Kind)

A Year Of Ideas: 365 sets of writing prompts
and exercises